*The Not-Dead and The Saved*
*and Other Stories*

KATE CLANCHY

# The Not-Dead and The Saved and Other Stories

PICADOR

First published 2015 by Picador
an imprint of Pan Macmillan
20 New Wharf Road, London N1 9RR
Associated companies throughout the world
www.panmacmillan.com

ISBN 978-0-330-53525-0

Visit **www.picador.com** to read more about all our books
and to buy them. You will also find features, author interviews and
news of any author events, and you can sign up for e-newsletters
so that you're always first to hear about our new releases.

*In memory of my beloved aunt,*

*Glenna Satterthwaite,*

*1935–2014.*

# Contents

*The Not-Dead and The Saved*
*and Other Stories*

# Aunt Mirrie and the Child

There is nothing wrong with the child. She says, thank you for coming, and goes to get her swimming kit. David appears from a doorway, nodding his approval.

Yes, he says. Thank you, Aunt Mirrie.

How odd to have a nephew of forty, even by marriage, and odder still to have him look it, holes in his jumper, ears furring up like a hobbit. Mirrie gives him a hug, knocking her large glasses on his chest.

David, she says, you smell of trouble.

Aunt Mirrie, he replies. What do you expect?

His red hair has faded, as it were overnight: all of him pale as if it were he who had been embalmed.

First you have to be a vicar, says Mirrie. Now this.

Oh, now, says David. The whole parish brought food.

He sits down on the stairs, gesturing at the hallway, the accretions of coats and mail and presents. There are dirty casserole dishes beside him, and an untouched quiche in foil. He picks it up and looks at it sorrowfully. Dusty, he says.

Not everyone can be practical in a crisis, says Aunt Mirrie. Tins you can buy. Time is the precious thing.

Every Saturday since Ruth got ill Mirrie has taken the child to the pool, and she does not see why this week should be different. They travel by small electric car, both in the front because there is no back, crammed up against the window. Aunt Mirrie has slidey wooden bead seats tied onto the real seats, and the child likes to roll the beads between her fingers on their taut white strings. She can't imagine what they are for.

It's March: a cold day. The child watches the battery gauge. The charge will get them the 3 miles from the house to Aunt Mirrie's club, and back again. Then the car has to be plugged into David's socket for 40 minutes while Mirrie has coffee, in order to get Mirrie the 10 miles home. Each week, when they get to the club, the child says, Aunt Mirrie, can't we plug it in here? And each week Mirrie says, no, darling, they make a silly fuss here, about their bill.

But, says the child now, her eyes on the gauge, 74%, Mummy always got cross when you plugged in the G-Wiz, too.

Yes, says Aunt Mirrie, but that wasn't because of the bill.

The child looks at Aunt Mirrie. Her arms come up high on the steering wheel and her thin hands grasp it: her little black eyes and pointy chin nod at the road. The child has long been sure she is an enchanted mouse. Why was it? she asks. Why was she so cross?

Because, says Aunt Mirrie, I was going to live and she was going to die. And look at me, a silly old lady, no one to care for, not even a cat. It makes me cross too.

She should have let you plug it in, said the child. All the same. You use the electricity to take me swimming. And you could get a cat if you wanted.

Child, said Aunt Mirrie. But it was only when she was ill. Chemo talking. We won't dwell on it.

The child can't remember when the chemo wasn't talking to Aunt Mirrie. But now they are at the club, and one must not talk to Aunt Mirrie during her parking which always takes a long, long, nudging time, like a Pekinese waddling round to make its bed. The car park is perched on the edge of a cliff. A ravine, says the child, gazing down the rhododendron- and paper-strewn descent to the sly brown river winking below.

Mirrie's pool is her treat. She worked all her life as a boring old secretary and had no one to spend money on, not like Daddy, so she can afford it. It was built a hundred years ago as a Turkish bath out of red granite and green tiles. It has the old notices still carved above the doors: *Hot Room*, *Cold Plunge*. But inside, now, it is mostly just a pool.

Another speciality is: the changing rooms don't have lockers, just pegs. This is because no one would steal anything here, they've all paid subscriptions. So you can just undress in a little cubicle with a curtain, then come out in your costume and hang everything up. Aunt Mirrie has also explained that it is safe to make two journeys: to hang up your dress, and go back for instance for your shoes; but the child is deeply conditioned by public pools and every time comes staggering out of her cubicle with all her clothes in a bundle, trainers on the top, tumbles it to the hot, tiled floor, and then spends five minutes hanging the lot up.

Mirrie lets her. She has placed her own coat on a peg, already, and now she is edging off her slip and inserting herself into her spotty costume, tugging the elastic panel over her tummy, tucking her breasts, little unbaked rolls, into the wired and padded cups. Her lucky breasts. She has perfect faith in them: she is sixty-eight and nothing has gone wrong yet, but she will take the test, as David asks.

When she comes out of the cubicle, the child is sitting sleek as a seal in her shining navy costume. Her ponytail is twisted up under a Lycra cap and on her lap is the black rubber brick she asked Mirrie to give her for her birthday, and which Mirrie went all the way to Lillywhites for. It is very heavy: exactly one kilo. A diving brick. Mirrie's pool is deep, deep as no modern pool is ever built, fifteen foot at the far end: you can dive.

I'm going to do lengths underwater, says the child. First.

Good, says Mirrie. There's plenty of room. For, look,

they are so early that there is only old Mr Jesbaum in the water, tugging his fat body end to end with his tiny, tyrannosaurus arms.

Aunt Mirrie swims on the surface, nose and pink cap and big round goggles out, long arms sweeping the meniscus, thin legs low and vague behind. Her lucky breasts point downwards, cradled in the water. Her sister Jessica got the unlucky breasts, though you wouldn't have known when they were first issued to both of them and Mirrie got the small parcel. Jessica thought hers were her fortune. She would pop them in a push-up bra and whizz them round a party like cupcakes on a tray.

In the green depths, pressed flat as a frog, swims the child. There are 11 tiles between Aunt Mirrie and the child at the shallow end, and 29 at the deep end. The child knows that when she swims down the pool she is also swimming down the cliff, because that is how the pool is built, cunningly into the side of the ravine. There is a stripe of blue tiles 9 tiles down. It starts at the bottom of the shallow end and laps the green pool like a ribbon. You can keep your goggled eye on it to mark your way to the depths. Egyptian blue. Malachite. Archaeology.

Mirrie remembers Jessica: snapping black eyes and cashmere sweaters, breasts purposeful as gun turrets. Not for long. Divorced, divorced, was Jessica, and chop, chop gone, her pretty breasts, and Jessica dead at thirty-three. That was how it was, then. But at least Jessica's breasts had fun. Ruthie had scowled resentfully over the great shelf of her chest as if it were a shop counter, and she the cross Saturday girl, too clever for the job. No parties and push-up bras for Ruth's breasts, no lace and décolletage: they were draped in long tunics like furniture under dust sheets; they went to meetings and protests in heavy disguise until the day they too were cut off.

The child has swum 6 lengths under water. Now she starts her diving. Over and again she ducks from the surface, swims down, pulls the black brick from the bottom, paddles it to the air, lifts it out in a victory salute, then lets it drop again, heavy and slow. Sometimes, when she dives down, Aunt Mirrie is above her, akimbo as an angel: sometimes, when she comes up, Aunt Mirrie is there, waving a little mouse wave.

Mirrie is thinking about Ruthie. It is easier to do so now she is finally dead. Now she is out of the maelstrom of new drug names and different dates; out of the maze of hospital corridors and visiting hours gone wrong. Now she will never shout at Mirrie again.

Now one can think, for example, that it was always difficult to say the right thing to her, not just at the end. That even when she was a little child she was never smiling and complaisant like this child; you could never so much as take her shopping or compliment her school work without a scowl; and that this was not perhaps her fault, or Mirrie's in fact, but Jessica's, who was not a good parent because she always had to be the child herself.

The child is doing something new: she drops the brick, then swims underneath it as it flip flops down, and catches it before it lands. She lies kicking on the bottom with it clutched to her chest and counts, 1, 2, 3 . . . Her blood is strong in her ears. 8 is not enough. She must get to 10. The child does not think she will grow to have a flat bum like Aunt Mirrie's, or wide hips, or a gap between her thighs. She does not plan on having breasts like her mother's, hefty as pillows, then gone. She will stay lithe as a snake at the bottom of the pond.

There must, thinks Mirrie, rowing the boat of herself over the sunk shape of the child, have been another Ruthie, one she could never know because who could Mirrie ever be to Ruth but Jessica's sister, with all that meant? Mirrie turns at the shallow end, breathes, swims on. And this other Ruth was a wife to David who is a nice, nice man, a treasure for all the religious freakery, and also mother to this child, so compact and tranquil and good. This unseen Ruthie must have talked of things other than global apocalypse and plastic bags. She must have smiled because her child smiles.

At the bottom of the pool the child, brick to chest, stiff as a tomb figure, listens to the pistons of her heart and counts. The sun comes out behind a high window and sends a shaft of light into the pool, lighting the water, gold, green, and at that moment Aunt Mirrie swims above the child and between them appears a shadow shape and for both of them it is the shape of Ruth in her zip-up bag, ready to be moved to the mortuary.

The child bursts to the surface, and clutches the green edge of the deep end, breathing. Mirrie joins her. Mr Jesbaum gets out at the other end and waddles to the changing room and they are alone.

Aunt Mirrie says: Your mum was angry with me because of her mum, my sister.

She died, says the child. Before I was born.

Yes, says Aunt Mirrie. And she ought not to have done that. She ought not.

She couldn't help it, says the child. It's a gene.

Yes, says Aunt Mirrie. No. But she should still have said sorry.

Didn't she? asks the child.

No, says Aunt Mirrie. They are both holding on to the green edge of the pool, white knuckled. The water laps their shoulders. Mirrie says: When Jessica was dying, she sent Ruthie away. Your mum. With her dad and his new wife.

Mummy's step-mother, says the child. She didn't like her.

No, says Aunt Mirrie. She wasn't a nice woman. He wasn't a nice man.

Was it for a long time? asks the child.

All the time Jessica was ill, says Aunt Mirrie. All that time Jessica didn't see Ruthie. And then she died.

Why didn't you stop her? asks the child. Grandma?

Aunt Mirrie doesn't know. Because it was a hard thing to say and she was ill? Because Jessica was her little sister and she'd always babied her? Because it was different, then?

Maybe, said the child, you thought Grandma would get better? I thought Mummy would get better, all the way till she died. I couldn't help it.

Yes, said Aunt Mirrie. That's right. Child. There was that.

The child puts her arms above her head and sinks herself to the bottom of the pool. She crosses her legs and sits briefly on the bottom. She has solved a mystery. She shoots to the surface. Aunt Mirrie is still clinging to the edge.

I knew the G-Wiz didn't need charging, really, says the child.

No, says Aunt Mirrie.

Could you have had Mummy to stay with you? asks the child. When she was little. When Grandma died?

Yes, says Aunt Mirrie, I could. I could, for all she didn't like me.

Didn't she ever like you? asks the child.

No, says Aunt Mirrie. But really, what of that? I was the adult. I knew how it all was. I could have done better. Your mother had every right to be angry with me.

The child says: Don't cry.

Oh, says Aunt Mirrie. But it's good to cry. And a

swimming pool is a good place. No one will ask you about your red eyes.

But in the changing room, their eyes are not so red. The child's freckles stick out as they always do after swimming: a frequency graph; cells on a Petri dish, swarming. She pulls off her rubber cap, and Aunt Mirrie combs out her hair, which is very long and dark red, she gets it from her father. Mirrie says it is very good hair, very strong, and will do her a long time. She should not let anyone say it is coarse or twit her on its colour. It will take all kinds of dyes, it will take fifty years of fashion-able cuts, even the very difficult directional bob (the child does not know what this is), and when it greys, she can make herself over as a convincing blonde because she has the green eyes for it. Look.

In the mirror, Jessie smiles.

# Bride Hill

My husband has Alzheimer's disease and my daughter does not believe me.

If I ring her and say, he went out for ham and milk and he came back with an empty bag, she will say, oh, I do that all the time.

Or if I say, for example, he took the bus into town and then he walked back, she will say, that's the healthy option, and if I say no, it was because he couldn't remember where the bus stop was, she will laugh and say: he's a philosopher, what do you expect?

I say, today he bought the *Guardian* twice, and there are six reels of twine in the shed when we only need one, and she says, Mum, you have to take into account that you're both retired, now. You're in the house together, now, all the time. You're just *noticing* stuff. Normal stuff. Why don't you come here for a week, help out with the kids, give yourself some space? But, as she predicts, I do not do this.

*Ordinary*, says my daughter, over and over, *normal*.

And of course it is *ordinary* for him to walk past the bus stop, *normal* for him to carry several full paper bags, or one empty one, and, yes, he has always liked shopping at the ironmonger's. I am a materialist, after all, he will say to the neighbours, or their too-young children, and then he will explain at length what this means, philosophically. In the shed, everything is in order, to look at. Everything is *normal*. It would take me, the nagging, fault-finding wife, to notice the extra twine, or that he has twice left the shovel in the compost, and once on top of the car.

I think my daughter thinks we are too young for such a problem. I think that because Jeff is sixty-eight and I am sixty-five; because we are thin, brown, white-haired people with gold-framed glasses; because we are the *active retired* and favour a practical style of dress in modern fabrics such as fleece, and colourful lace-up shoes and walking trousers which we buy from a German catalogue; because we often undertake long walks using Scandinavian metal poles: my daughter thinks our brains are equally wiry, equally up to the long coast-walks of the mind.

Or, she thinks I am making it up. My daughter has always thought I grudge her. It's not the war, my daughter says. There isn't rationing. My daughter's business, from the day she could get out the front gate on her own, the moment she got her fat hand on the hot tap, has been to defy me, to run the deep bath, to get first the Parma violets and then the cheap clothes and the boyfriends and now the four-by-four and the wide-screen telly for herself, despite me. I believe she discusses my phone calls with her friends, among whom it is well known that wives bear grudges, wives like me, *who gave everything up*, unlike the wives of Jennifer's generation who apparently *have it all*.

But if jobs are so important, qualifications, careers, then at least my daughter should respect my scientific training, when she has none herself. She often rolls her eyes at the antiquity of my degree, says times have moved on since sixty-five Mum, but in fact I have read about the new thinking in the area of Alzheimer's and looked things up on the computer at which I am a dab hand. I have tried to bring my daughter up to date with my research. I rang and said, Jennifer, do you know what the *hippocampus* is? And she sighed and guessed, *horse field*, Latin was one of her O levels, and when I said no, hippocampus meant sea horse, she said: and you say *Dad*'s senile?

Well. This sort of banter is part of our relationship. Many mothers and daughters behave like this. There is no point in taking offence or in writing a letter with a diagram enclosed because my daughter does not do letters. She calls them snail mail. She is incapable of buying a stamp.

So, after a day or two, I ring again, but this time I tell her, without preamble: Jennifer, the hippocampus is part of the brain. It is the shape of a sea horse, the size of a sea horse, has the very shine of that primitive marine creature, particularly when pickled, imagine a sea horse coiled underneath the cerebral cortex – and Jennifer says, OK, Mum, I'm imagining the sea horse. And?

Well, I say, the hippocampus is old, like the sea horse. Primitive, like the sea horse. All mammals have one.

In the brain? says Jennifer.

In the brain, I say, in the bottom of the brain.

What does it do? says Jennifer, sounding marginally interested.

Well, I say, the cells there have Neural Plasticity, that means they can make patterns. They have Long-Term Potentiation. LTP. The patterns can go into your long-term memory.

That's nice, says Jennifer. And?

Well, I say, in Alzheimer's, the hippocampus often goes first. The neurons become weighed down by plaques. They shrink. Their proteins tangle. *Sclerotic*, is the word.

Right, says Jennifer. The sea horse is sclerotic. Shrunk. Like the dried kind. You brought me one of those once, from Italy.

And then, I say, when the hippocampus is sclerotic, when it can't light up its neurons, there is a traffic jam in the brain. A blockage.

An outage, says Jennifer, and there is a scratching

noise at her end. I imagine her jotting down a shopping list, thinking of something else, not listening.

And so, I say, because there isn't a pathway, you can't process new experiences through to your long-term memory. You can't lay down new memories.

Umph, says Jennifer.

Your father, Jennifer, I say. The ham, Jennifer, I say. The milk. The bus stop. The empty bag.

And Jennifer makes a scoffing noise like the paper bag punched and says, Wikipedia is a terrible thing.

But the next day, she calls back. She says does he do Sudoku it's good for the brain and I say, of course not, his subject is philosophy. And then she says: Look, the kids are back at school next week. I'll come over on Monday, and we'll take Dad to Bride Hill. And of course that is a lovely idea.

But over the five days before Monday, I think about Jennifer's choice of picnic location, and review the available web-literature on the subject of the hippo-campus, and realize that the picnic, like for example my grandchildren's extravagant christening parties, is nothing but a trap designed by my daughter to make me look dry, over-analytical, wrong. For Bride Hill is more than a nearby Ancient Monument appropriate to family outings: it is a maze, a ritual maze cut in the chalk. Jenni-fer, I am certain, has been reading of the performances of rats in mazes, and about the map-forming functions of the hippocampus thus discovered, and in her usual, hazy, unscientific manner has concluded that if her father, Jeff, who indeed has grown whiskery and long-nosed with the years, is placed in the maze and succeeds in finding the path to the centre, she, Jennifer, will have successfully demonstrated to me, her stupid mother with the out-dated science degree, that there is nothing sclerotic about his hippocampus and that he does not have Alzheimer's Disease.

Once I have realized this intention, I strongly consider, over a period of three days, the possibility of telephoning my daughter and telling her that I have rumbled her. Also, that her test is based on a false principle. The hippocampus *does* form maps in our heads, but as a tool, like a compass or a sextant. The hippocampus is not a plan-chest of maps. That plan-chest lives in our long-term memories, and lots of Jeff's maps are still fine, which is why he can walk to the ironmonger's. There is a map of Bride Hill there too, I should think, for we have been there so often. The bus stop, on the other hand, which moved this year, is beyond him because he cannot make a new map of it because his hippocampus is sclerotic. So the bus stop is the fair test, not the maze: but how can I ring and tell Jennifer that? She will simply deny the whole thing. On Sunday, I find the lawnmower out, abandoned on the half-cut lawn, but still, I do not call.

And so it is that on the Monday I put on the table several things which are in Jeff's long-term memory, already, things that do not need to go through the hippocampus and its LTP cells to be recognized and loved: the tartan thermos flask, the sandwiches, in grease-proof paper and elastic bands, his red cagoule, the picnic mat. Then his daughter comes, fat and forty, freckled and smiling, and she is safely in Long Term too, mine and his. And if Jeff seems astonished, if he has forgotten the short-term arrangements for the picnic which I have gone over and over with him, well, we do not notice. Aren't we all surprised by joy? Isn't that what joy is?

So, Jennifer drives the car, Jeff sits in the front with his sun hat on, and I am in the back beside the baby-seat. Jennifer is wearing sunglasses and peers often to the left, checking the satnav. I thought you'd know the way, I say, and she says, no, now I have my TomTom, I can't remember anything, and Jeff, who really is on top form, says it's all marvellous and there is an argument to be made for smart machinery actually being part of our brain, that we are all semi-cyborgs and perhaps have been ever since we invented the pocket watch or indeed the hand-axe.

Jennifer is smiling, tapping the indicator with a polished nail, and I can tell she is thinking, not much wrong there, and I want to tell her: your dad does this. His chat-track about semi-cyborgs was processed in the hippocampus years ago, and now it lives in his long-term memory and he can get it out and use it, on cue. It's *now* that can't go through there, down through the pipes to Long Term. Ask him where we're going Jennifer, he'll make a joke, because he won't remember what you told him an hour ago. The *now* of you, Jennifer, with all the new layers of you that I hardly recognize myself, which shock me when I see you – your great womanish hips, those glasses, the lines when you frown – he won't remember it this evening. But how would I even start to say such a thing? She looks so harmlessly smug and cheerful, so apparently in charge. My daughter loves to drive.

We drive. It is so flat, hereabouts, we can see Bride Hill miles off: a round egg of gold downland, and the maze on it outlined in white like a thumbprint or a silicon chip. The lines are trenches, really, dug deep into the hill and filled with chalk. It must have taken Neolithic man a long, long time, and then, what did they do with it, what was it for? A sacred path? A mnemonic for a ritual? A tribal sign? No one knows, exactly, though there are barrows everywhere around, and the design, as Jeff will say in a moment, when he is prompted by the sight of it, retains its own potency.

Look Mum, says Jennifer, red kites. And I look up through the sunroof and there they are, so very many of them, wheeling directly above me in a spiral, like leaves whirling down a drain.

And then we are parking, and get out into the day, which is golden and bright. Jeff says, marvellous, simply marvellous, and Jennifer says it is, Dad, it is, and looks at him adoringly, as she always has, and she does not look at me. And suddenly I feel angry, and I let them go over the National Trust stile and up to the maze and sit down instead on the bench that has been thoughtfully provided for the elderly and infirm.

There's always a wind up here. I listen to the dry noise it makes through the high grass, and smell the hay and chalk smell which has passed through my hippocampus on the perhaps hundred times I have made this trip, and which now again releases my children for me: lounging teenagers leaning on the stile; ten-year-olds in flares, chasing each other; toddlers tumbling, fat in nappies. All of these children shadow Jennifer and Jeff up the hill and pace the pale tracks of the maze, and now Jeff the young father goes with them, his blunt dark fringe falling over his eyes, talking about the possible meanings of this pattern, about the perfectly simple, perfectly mathematical route he has worked out to the centre, and somewhere in my brain the complicated release mechanism of my love engages, and slowly, reluctantly, clicks.

I know what is happening to Jeff by my chart of gaps: by the spade not on the hook, the lawn not mown, by the empty bag. I have been telling them to Jenny so she too can shade them in, and also to confirm them to myself, because each lack is so small. If she would listen, I would tell her that that is how the hippocampus was found out too. Like anti-matter, and black holes, and the right solution for Sherlock Holmes: by its absence.

In 1953, the year I had a tonsillectomy, a surgeon called Scoville performed an experimental operation on a young man with terrible epilepsy. Scoville cut away most of the young man's hippocampus, and when he woke up after the operation, he no longer had epilepsy, but he was amnesic, and his amnesia was special: sea horse-shaped.

And so the young man became Patient HM, and he was studied. It was found: he could remember the first twenty-five years of his life well, but not the two before the operation; he could recognize people from his past, but no one new, not even Dr Brenda Milner, who was studying him, not however often she came. He could not remember new information: facts such as a new president, or a man landing on the moon, would surprise him each time he was told; but when Dr Milner asked him to join dots on a piece of paper into a star while he looked only in a mirror, he learned, over three days, to get quicker and better at the task. (HM retained, everyone agreed, his mild and agreeable personality: I would not be so relaxed about such a request, whatever had been removed from my brain.) No matter how many times he joined the dots, though, and however skilled he became, HM never remembered that he had done such a thing before: his *procedural* memory worked, in short, but not his *declarative* memory.

Declarative memory. The part of the mind that tells you where you are. My faithful butler, who declares, as

I stand up now, and walk to the mouth of the maze, that Madam may follow Jeff's Route if she turns first to the left, then counter-intuitively to the right. Jeff's declarative memory didn't do this, today, because his is no longer a good servant, but one who has taken to drink, one who takes unscheduled holidays, one who appears, dishevelled, in the middle of the night, talking nonsense at length.

Ahead of me, Jeff and Jennifer are making a game of it, leaping from path to path, recklessly, flinging up their arms. Their laughter is thin ribbons. I am sure they are lost.

I stick to my route, starting with the long swoop to the right. It's easy. I pace the thin path and think about Brenda Milner, itching in those terrible clothes we had in the fifties, the roll-on and stockings, patiently watching HM as he breathes over his mirror-drawing. Him with his pencil; her with her notepad, shading into the field of human knowledge the shape of the hippocampus: the temporal lobes, the declarative memory, the procedural memory. Like a memorial brass being rubbed onto paper with black wax: the banana shapes becoming feet; the scattered uprights, legs; and somewhere above the bag of the crotch, black commas turning into praying hands.

Jennifer and Jeff are sitting in the centre of the maze, now, a worn, grassy spot surrounded by white hooks of chalk. Jenny's head is up, her profile pulling clear of her flesh: she looks like a girl. Jeff is talking. The path takes me away from them, one more swoop, then back. I follow it.

HM's mother lived with him for twenty years after the operation. Twenty years growing further and further from his recognition, as if he were docked in 1953, and she passing away from him in a great ship. Did she dye her hair, or dress in forties suits, to remain more the mother he'd known from the first twenty-seven years of his life? I could do that, wear roll-ons, roll necks, hum along to The Shadows—

But I live here. And anyway, it wouldn't last. Alzheimer's isn't just the hippocampus: in time, the whole brain shrinks, the frontal lobes, the long-term memory, the procedural memory, and all the while, insistently, the brainstem remembers how to breathe.

When I arrive in the centre of the maze, no one congratulates me on solving the puzzle. Jeff doesn't even stop talking. It makes my point, do you see, he says, that a personality only exists in reaction to others, and always in a forward trajectory in time. I recognize the discourse: heaven, and the essential self. He says: what will you talk about in heaven? What will you do in a perfected world? And no one has ever given me a decent answer!

And suddenly I see that Jennifer is crying. I sit down beside her and pat the middle of her anoraked back, the place you touch when you mean to be kind. I hate to be right, in fact. And Jennifer sniffs and says, I think heaven is now, don't you think so, Mum?

Then we all sit on a while in the sun, and Jeff says again, it is so wonderfully warm. It is. If you shut your eyes, you could take it for real heat, the generative heat of spring. You could forget that September is just the afterglow of summer, the impression on the eyes after the candle is blown out.

# *Irene*

*(For Clare and Hilary Flenley)*

I was eight hours home from the hospital; three days
since the birth. It was the black middle of the night, and
I was standing at the bottom of my stairs, holding the
banister.

There was my auntie, perched on my sofa, singing to
the baby in her old, old, voice:

*Oh you cannae push yer granny off a bus . . .*

It's only Irene, dear, she said, meeting my eye, no
need to look affrontit. But all I was thinking was: where
had she found that blanket to swaddle him, the one I
thought I'd lost, blue, satin binding, hollow-knit? And:
how had she tucked the corners in, so neat, like a parcel?

John went back to London, I said, thickly. Because it
was him, maybe, had given her the key.

Is that so? said Irene. I made you a coffee.

Hot milk, with bitter speckles of Nescafé. I hadn't
drunk such a thing in years. The cup wasn't mine, either

– thick and white, with a saucer. Crawford's, that's where it came from: Crawford's coffee shop, 1980, me skiving out of school with my pals. People smoked on buses, then, and this was a cappuccino.

I thought you'd be wanting a woman about the place, said Irene. Now the wee gentleman's here.

Irene shifted the baby so he was in profile to me, his neck on her arm, his tiny folded nose and chin grave as a pharaoh's. He looks like you, I said. Irene's nose was hooked over her mouth, too. She looked at the baby, pushed out her teeth, pushed them back and clicked her tongue in agreement, pleased.

And she's surprised, your mum, she said to the sleeping baby. But we're not surprised, are we, the precious poppet?

Irene had seventeen years on my mother, they were always saying that. She was so old, now. Her perm was rigid as the Queen's, and she had no calves, just bone. Her brown stockings were loose, her court shoes like coffins. The baby's legs were the same, they didn't have any muscle. He was loose in my hand as washing, and I couldn't sleep for the worry of holding him up.

When you've finished that coffee, said Irene, you should go off to bed. I'll sit up with the little one, if that's all right by you.

I need to feed him, I said. But I didn't really want to. I was all scooped out inside, like a breakfast egg, and I had fourteen stitches across my belly. Irene waved a bottle at me – a strange, narrow bottle with a rigid pink nipple.

I'll give him a nice drink. Never you worry, she said.

I went back upstairs, remembering the bottle. It was the one I'd fed my Tiny Tears with, the one I'd dropped down a grating at the bottom of our tenement stair in 1968. Irene was singing, again:

*You can push yer ither granny off a bus,*
*You can push yer ither granny,*
*For she's yer mammy's mammy –Ye can push yer*
*ither granny off a bus . . .*

What a terrible thing to say, she murmured to the baby. Isn't that a terrible thing to do to yer granny? The speed those buses go, round George Square.

When I woke up, Irene was gone. She'd left a cigarette end, pressed out in the glass votive candle holder John had given me, and the baby, still swaddled in the blanket. I didn't mind about the candle holder – who would I be votive to? – and the baby was easier to feed, wrapped, but I couldn't fold him back in after I did the nappy. I called John, and asked about it, and he said I shouldn't swaddle, babies needed to be free, so I stopped and just stared at the baby on the nappy table. His little arms, his spread legs – I'd sprawled like that for hours and hours in front of everyone, trying to push him out, and it hadn't done any good.

*

Came to the birth, did he? said Irene. This was daytime. The baby was on her yellow tweed lap and her bony knees were far apart. I remembered being a little girl and the dread of accidentally looking up there, past the pantyhose hammock to the nameless black cavity.

Yes, I said. Of course.

Aye, well, said Irene, modern times. But it's a terrible idea if you ask me. How do you expect to have any more?

John doesn't want any more, I said. He's got two already. Ten and fourteen.

Och darling, said Irene, he's never *married*? I was surprised, how sympathetic she sounded. It gave me a watery feeling in my guts, and hot tears in my eyes, but those were wobbly times when I cried at anything. Post-partum, that's what they call it. In parts. Parted from yourself.

No, I said, he's divorced. But you know, you don't divorce *children*.

Oh, it's been known, said Irene.

No, I said. Not John. You see, he has very high standards.

Very high standards, said Irene to the baby. That's what we like. She shoved a saucer at me: a Tunnock's teacake, in its stripy bell-skirt of foil, but I just needed to go to sleep. Something was bubbling in my pasta pan and there was a strange smell: like my grandmother's dark little flat when I was being minded and she had the wash on. Soap soup.

I gathered up the baby's wee things, said Irene. Popped them on the stove. That'll get the stains out.

When I woke up, the Babygros and muslins were cold in their pot, and I rinsed them and pegged them out. I took the baby out to the garden with me in his car seat, and he opened his marbly blue eyes and looked at me for a short while. I was getting used to him, a little. My stitches were healing. *So this is what you do*, I thought. *Pegging out, and you take the baby along.* John came.

Did you not make him tea? said Irene, as his car backed out of my drive.

He'll get some at home.

Och. But he's living on his own.

Not exactly. He has a flat at the top of the family house. In Highgate.

His mother's house?

No. His wife's house. Ex-wife's. And, in response to Irene's stony stare: She's a barrister, he's a musician. So when the marriage came to an end, he couldn't afford a place. And he didn't want to leave his kids. So there he is. It all works very well.

Does it indeed? said Irene. Did you ever hear of such a thing? *Marriage came to an end.* (She said this in a phoney English accent.) My my. Modern times, eh?

I was quiet for a bit and Irene said: My Donald was married. Aye. Did your mother never tell you?

No.

Aye, well. That's your mother for you. Scarlet Auntie Irene, eh?

But I couldn't remember my mother mentioning Irene at all.

Irene put on the racing and we both watched it while the baby sucked. There was a horse called Bit-on-the-Side and Irene kept saying: My money's on that one. Eh? What do you say? Let's bet the house. Eh? Eh? I fell asleep in the end. Irene left me three cheese scones, their tops shiny with egg.

Night-time. I was emailing John. He was on tour but he wrote to me every evening, lovely encouraging messages. Irene appeared, in her quilted nylon dressing gown.

Here ye are, lassie, she said. It was a tumbler of whisky, no ice. She was clutching one herself, dark as treacle in her horny hand.

I was just a slip of a thing when I met Donald, she said. I was the Saturday girl in his shop.

What sort of shop?

Shoes. Och, you remember. A grand big shop. Sauchiehall Street.

I did remember: plate glass, fold-up ladders, a smell of leather and mahogany. Irene worked there till she retired. Uncle Donald had polished oxfords and a shining bald head.

Did you take me, I said, to the Kibble Palace? Because I could see those oxfords against the marble edging in the hot-house. There was a tiny creeping plant and a little black-and-white laminated sign saying *Mind Your Own Business*. Funny. A funny name.

Irene nodded. Just the once, she said. You were awful good.

I'd had a blue knitted dress. The memory telescoped itself back to a photo of me in that dress, a Kodachrome photo, orangey with a dark frame to it. It was on the dresser in Irene's flat, a place we hardly ever went.

Then he died, said Irene. Donald. And I couldnae go to the funeral. I stepped out with him for thirty-five years. All my good years, and no one to tell. D'you see, lassie? D'you see what I'm saying?

I swivelled back to the screen. It had switched to *saver*, and the shifting pattern was passing through Irene's pale reflection, pixelating and dispersing her again and again like rain swept from a windscreen.

John isn't anything like that, I said. But Irene had gone.

The next time John came, he said he thought I'd made Irene up, that she was just an excuse for me eating sweets and smoking. We both laughed at that. But how could it be me, I said, ironing the muslins? Or saving up butter-wrappers to grease the skillet for scones?

John was just on his way out the door, holding his overnight bag, but he put it down and asked me, in a very serious voice, if I was all right.

Don't go back to London, then, I said. If you're worried. Stay here, and cook.

There was a long pause. Then John picked up his bag and said: I just wish you'd use the baby sling. Get out a bit more.

It breaks my back, I said. I'd already told him.

Go to yoga, then, he said. Get to work on those stomach muscles. Start thinking positive.

He wasn't being unkind. There was Irene with the home-made tablet, sticky and brown in its tray.

In a fair hurry, your man, she said, sucking. She'd left her teeth out.

Judith – that's his daughter – she needs one-to-one time. She's got issues round the baby.

Oh, said Irene, Issues! She said it like a sneeze, and we both laughed our heads off. I took another square of tablet.

You know, I said, this is what breast milk tastes like. So sweet, it's shocking.

Och, said Irene, you never did taste it, did you?

Yeah, I said. Why not? It's natural. Full of antibiotics.

Like picking your nose, said Irene.

But when John and I had our big row – the one which started with the yoga class versus regular naps, and ended with him stamping on my scones; the one when he said he *just couldn't do a conventional bourgeois marriage again, hadn't he been quite clear?* and *nuclear families explode* and I said I was *ON MY OWN THEN* and he said I was a *con-trick*, and I'd *pretended to be someone different*, and I realized that was *TRUE* but I hadn't done it on purpose – I couldn't find Irene at all. Someone else was cleaning up the crumbs when I came back in the house, someone in a dark skirt, down on her knees.

I can do that, I said.

You can not, said the person. Sit you down like the fine lady you are.

I'm not a fine lady.

She stopped, turned to me. A heavy, jowly face, newsprint-coloured: me on a bad morning, in a steamed mirror. No, she said. You're a Jezebel. A hot wee whore. And yon's yer bastard.

That was the only time I thought I was seeing things. It was the feeling of a misstep on a steep stair, or when a car misses you by a whisker – that whooshing sound, that wall of air. I walked out smartly and closed the door, sat down on the low chair, put the baby on to feed, but the woman kept on cleaning, banging about with brooms. I watched her through the frosted-glass kitchen door for some time.

You're to fuck off, I called out at last, but my voice lacked conviction. I didn't want to disturb the baby, slack in my arms.

That night, Irene was back, in her quilted gown, passing the saucer. A shortbread finger, just the one. She looked terrible – her hair deflated, her skin yellow and dry. Mummified.

Your man's hightailed it, then? she said.

He's taking some space, I said. Irene nodded.

Lassie, she said. You need to call your mother.

I can't do that, Irene, I said.

Now, said Irene, Jean's a difficult wee woman and I am not denying it. But, hinny, does she know about the bairn?

Irene. I told her I was pregnant. She cut me off. You know that.

But does she know he's really here, now? The wee laddie.

I didn't call her when he was born. No.

Och, said Irene. But it's six weeks. He's grown up already. Think what she's missed! You have to give her another chance.

No. I said. I don't. I really don't.

You're a wicked wee bitch, not to tell her. So you are. After all she's done for you.

What did she do for me?

Och darling, said Irene, pointing at the baby at my breast, the swaddle, night light. She did all this.

So I called my mother, and we had a long and startling conversation. I thought it would be the last of Irene, but she was back by the cot, that same afternoon. I saw no point beating round the bush.

My mother says, I said. That you're dead.

Your mother and I never did see eye to eye, said Irene. She was crocheting, I noticed, a new thing. Mercerized cotton, bone hook, bone fingers.

She said you died last month. Cancer of the oesophagus.

Jean, said Irene, hooking a stitch, always did believe what suited herself best.

Irene, I said.

Aye. She was away out the door in that skirt. She thought she looked grand.

They've gone through your papers up there. Mum says maybe you're not her big sister after all. She says maybe you're her mother.

Aye, said Irene. Well. You can see how the confusion might have arisen. Living as we did, and things as they were. It was different then, lassie. You've no idea.

Are you, though? I said. Are you her mother?

Irene was wavering in front of my eyes, resolving into textures: flannel sheet, frosted glass, hollow-knit blanket with satin binding.

A mother's the woman who does the work, said Irene. Does the night feed, boils the clothes. My mother told me that. The work. And that wasnae me. Not back then, when I was a lassie. It wasnae me. I was never a mother.

My tongue was swelling and watering in my mouth. It wanted to say something Scottish, but it had forgotten the shapes.

You were so, I muttered. Irene. You were so. But now

there was only the crochet hook by the cot, and a tiny boat of knotted cotton, and a curl of unspooled yarn.

It needed my mother to identify the boat as the sole of a blue bootee. She took it in hand, and finished the pair, and tugged them on David's fine plump feet one sunny morning. He waved them above his head, gaa-ing with pleasure. There now, she said, surveying her handiwork. The precious poppet. And won't Granny be proud, pushing you out in the pram?

# Black Bun

But, said Sandra, if Archie hadn't wanted to invite Ruairi, he should have said so from the start. She was brushing her hair in the triple mirror, target of both new, directional, spotlights. She had on her new dress: dark green, all the way to the floor. Steel reflection: silver brush. She added: This was hardly the time to kick up a fuss.

Archie was in the shadows by the fitted wardrobe, unmanned in his kilt and hairy knee socks. He said: But we didn't invite him, surely.

It's a family party, said Sandra, tutting lipstick onto her mouth. And he's your cousin.

Adopted cousin, said Archie. He isn't blood.

How is that different? asked Sandra. She had quite the posh accent, these days: *How* was turbo charged; *different* was a small aircraft in the next field. She picked up her bomb of *L'Air du Temps*. For heaven's sake, she said, we thought of adopting, after Christine. Are you saying that child wouldn't have been family? She aimed at her neck, and fired.

Archie wriggled his woolly toes in the new shag-pile. I was thinking of Jenny, he said. And the children. I was thinking of them.

But Jenny and the children are coming, said Sandra. They've a lift arranged.

Exactly, said Archie, and how is that normal? Would you say? Coming to a party with your divorced dad? A *Hogmanay* party with all the family there? What will the weans make of it? And he sat down heavily on the bed.

It'll be 1978 tomorrow, said Sandra. Modern times.

Well, said Archie, gazing at his new kilt jacket where it hung on the wardrobe door. (Purple velvet, corded round the cuffs, Sandra's idea, he wasn't sure.) Aye, but all the same. Poor wee Jenny.

Sandra said: Jenny is *fine* with being divorced. She is *grand* with it actually. Better than waiting up all hours to see if Ruairi's coming home or chasing his fancy women all over Newton Mearns. A *fine* arrangement.

Archie picked at the quilted bedcover. It was *olive*. He'd heard Sandra say so on the phone. *A keynote colour*, that's what she'd said, *all over the house*. So it was. All sorts of things were mud coloured. Skirting boards. The toilets. The shag pile – like a ploughed field. Not that he'd said anything. He'd given Sandra a free hand with the paint and the soft furnishings. Not many wives had as much. She didn't say that on the phone.

Ruairi, said Sandra, comes to see the children all the time, he's a lamb with them, they get on grand.

But, said Archie, Jenny lives with her *parents*.

Sandra stood up. So do you, she said. I'm away to see if your mother's OK right now. And she marched out.

Which was a foolish, a bafflingly foolish thing to say. Archie rubbed his furry knees. How could there be any comparison between Jenny, returned like an errant child to her parents' house in Glasgow, and Archie, moving out here to take over his grandfather's house, his *family* house, and care for his aging mother? The money, for a start. Look at the accounts of it (Archie was an accountant). Everyone knew Jenny's parents had had to throw out an extension to accommodate her, and that poor Sandy had postponed his retirement to pay the school fees for her boys; whereas Archie, Archie had bought this house, fair and square, and he had paid off his sister's share in advance of the will, and he had paid the same all over again to make the new wing for Mum.

No, Sandra was making an excuse, that was all. Archie pulled the shoe trees out his brogues. It was the same as ever: another excuse for Ruairi. Ever since they were boys together, this had been going on. Ruairi on their grandad's knee, where no one sat, because it was sad he'd no dad of his own, and Archie should be kind. Ruairi playing his trumpet after lunch, or singing a wee song, because wasn't it lovely he had a talent when he was an orphan with only Flora in all the world. Ruairi with the Hornby set at Christmas, because that was the sort of foolish present mums bought with no dad to guide them, and Flora was foolish to start with, it was foolish to adopt a child like that, when you'd been ill and you were on your own. They'd never have let her do it except the child was a dark one, touch of the tar brush, but maybe it wasn't going to show, maybe he'd grow up OK; he was awful handsome, the dark only showing in his eyes, in his thick, flat, India Ink hair.

Archie's new brogues had fancy laces with fringed leather ends. They had special flaps to pull over the bow. They were stiff and brown and fiddly and smelt in their depths of shit. Archie sighed over them, bent double. He remembered Scally, his own Skye terrier, following Ruairi everywhere. He remembered the smelly wee beast even being allowed to sleep on his bed when he came to stay, and all Archie's wee pals and Catriona from over the street playing only Ruairi's games for a whole six weeks. They were stupid games, all nonsense about treasure and pretending. But Ruairi was that bit younger than Archie, said his mother, Ruairi was only nine and his poor mum was having Chemo and who else did he have in the world?

Archie stood up and peered at himself, blurred, red-haired, fattening, in Sandra's long cruel mirror. He remembered Catriona asking, what was the address to write Ruairi a letter, and the dog howling in the spare room. The despatch of the dog, his own Scally, for Christ's sake, in a special dog hamper bought for the purpose, a few months later when Flora died and Ruairi went to live for good with Gran and Grandad in the big house, in this house, and Archie wasn't to mind because he hardly bothered with the creature, and think what a difference it would make to Ruairi when the lid burst open and out came the wee bright-eyed thing.

Well. The dog was long dead, and now Archie had the house. He stood, and stretched his arms out into it: the velvety depths of the bedroom, the long, low spaces beyond. He pulled them back in his fists: the shadows, the wide grave turns of the corridors, the acres of mid-winter dark outside. Bungalow. The word bounced in his mind as it always had, like a tennis ball over a mile of parquet. All of it his, and tonight was his party.

He'd walked through the whole house this evening, checking every inch of carpet re-laid, every window renewed and double glazed. Sandra had been all for adding another floor. She said, a new bedroom suite for themselves, and a bit of special space for Christine, to compensate her, for the girl had wanted to stay on in Glasgow, spend every weekend with her friends. She was fourteen, next birthday. But Archie wouldn't have a bar of it. He wanted the floors and the corridors wide and flat, the way they were when he was a boy, and the lounge big as an airport, and that's what he got. Christine had got her bedroom and en suite – she was in it now, he had no doubt, showing her new grand dress to her pal from Pollock Shields, prinking herself in the wall of mirrors. Sandra had her new kitchen, walnut look with waste disposal unit, every surface of it just now covered with cling-filmed dishes: smoked salmon on rye; scraps of haggis on oatcakes which was a disgusting idea, like so many wee cowpats; and, behind it all, the black bun, that solid mass of dried fruit, breadcrumbs and liquor, round as an igloo, two foot across.

They had folded away the dining table for the party, laid the chairs against the wall, opened up the panels to the lounge. Now the sheer green expanse of triple-pile carpet rolled all the way to the French windows, fine as a fairway on a spring day. Archie patted the dance records piled by the Bang & Olufsen, poured himself a whisky from the bottles lined up on the new black ash sideboard. He could remember standing in this room as a boy, and Ruairi saying, apropos of nothing, showing off to his grandmother, that he loved that room, it was *full of sky*, and getting a hug for it – and then that he loved the parquet because it was *like mars bars*, and getting another. Well, the parquet was gone. Archie had had it cut up and burnt in a bonfire outside the garage, and if Ruairi was coming here tonight, at least he would see that. Archie tossed whisky on his tonsils. *Comeuppance*, that was the word on his mind.

Archie, said Sandra, from the doorway. She swished across the room, took the glass from his hand, and hissed (for they were both mindful of the wee friend from Pollock Shields). It's your mother. You'll have to help.

It had been Archie who hadn't wanted to pay the nurse for tonight. Not triple rate. But now, as he swung through the double doors to the new wing, he caught the whiff of shit, rich as raisins and whisky, and was sorry. In the bedroom, though, everything looked orderly and his mother's new dress was laid across her bed. It was a lovely dress for an old lady: black velvet bodice, tartan skirt. You couldn't beat Sandra for a daughter-in-law, that was for sure. She'd taken Grace for a wash-and-set too. It was too bad of the old lady to be standing ungrateful in her slip in the middle of the room.

Will she not put the dress on? he asked Sandra, who was wearing her apron over her green dress, he saw, and rubber gloves. There was a washing-up bowl of soapy water on the carpet.

It's not my dress, Grace quavered. It's not. She stole my dress, she added, pointing to Sandra, and she's wearing it herself. She tells you she isn't but she is. She's a thief.

Sandra's lips were tightly pursed, and she was shaking her head slowly from side to side. There was, Archie now saw, a great streak of crap down the back of his mother's slip.

I'll dress her, said Sandra, but you'll have to do the bathroom. I'm drawing a line, Archie. A line.

Did the rest go in the pan? whispered Archie, but Sandra merely tossed her head towards the door, and in he went.

The smell was very strong in here. Archie reminded himself that his mother had looked after her dead husband's father, his own grandad, in this house for five years before finally he died, and he probably shat himself plenty. He reminded himself that if she hadn't done that, the house would most likely have been left to Ruairi, because, till the very end of his days, none of Ruairi's failures counted for anything to the old man. All the same, thought Archie. Bloody hell. He opened the wee frosted window, took a deep breath of freezing damp air, heard the rattle of soaking trees.

Then he turned and saw something furry in the bath. He shouted out, Sandra, there's a rat in here!

But it was his mother's evening purse, really, the mink one with the gold clasp. A turd had been stuffed inside, but it was too big, it was overflowing. And, now Archie came to look around him, he could see the bathroom was covered with shit too, it was just disguised, because of the direction of the directional spot, and because the suite was *olive*.

Archie took off his fancy purple jacket, hung it up, and pulled on the flowery overall the nurse used to wash Grace. He found the rubber gloves on the back of the U-bend. He washed the purse as best he could in the toilet bowl, but there was even more of the stuff than you'd think, it was all matted into the fur and the silk lining, and he held it under the water and thought: this can never be any use to anyone but what is the way out?

44

In the other room, Grace was crying the way he remembered Christine doing, when she was wee, and Sandra was teaching her to sleep. Sandra said in her sharp, dog-training voice: *I am not a thief. Archie is not a thief. We are in your house to take care of you.* And then, after a squeal that sounded honestly not human, more like a deer shot in the woods, another burst of Sandra: *I cannae put up with this, I cannae, and Archie cannae either, we just cannae, wheesht yersel'*.

So Archie knew he had to do something. He grabbed the purse out of the toilet bowl and threw it out the window, out into the bushes. Then he grasped the green smelly toilet cleaner and squirted it wildly round the bath and followed it with hot water from the shower head and squirted and scrubbed until the whole room stank of chlorine and synthetic pine. He washed his hands with the gloves on, then tore them off and washed again. He sat down on the toilet. The purse would freeze out there, he thought. Then, when it was frozen and didn't stink, it could be picked up and be, not burnt, that wouldn't work, but disposed of, somehow. Wrapped in black bin bags, maybe, sealed with masking tape. A jiffy bag. He would nip by in the early morning, and sort it.

We're good now, said Sandra. And Archie went back in the bedroom and found his mother sitting on her bed, with her hands clasped in front of her, and her face impassive; sunk, as it so often was these days, in folds like an elderly Pekinese. The dress covered her neatly, its taffeta skirt sticking up like a little girl's.

She's got turd under her nails, said Sandra, but I'm past caring. Sandra looked awful. Great shadows under her eyes, tears in them. Archie wanted to make up with her. Folk'll think it's black bun, he said. And Sandra giggled.

Come on, said Archie to his wife. She'll sit here an hour now. She's got her church face on. We'll get a wee whisky. We'll come back for her. He stuck out his arm to Sandra, like asking her to dance. Hook on, he said, and she did, and they were almost out the door when the old lady, sticking her lip out as far as it could go, said sepulchrally, informatively: Aye, you think you're going to get away with it. I know the truth, I know what you stole.

But it had all been done fair and square. Archie had even let Ruairi keep the old man's golf clubs, and anyway, where else was he expecting Grace to live, when her husband was long dead and the bungalow was her home?

Sandra gave Archie a wee tug. She's wandering, she said. When your sister gets here, then we'll bring her out. And, with a moment of resistance like a hoop skirt being pulled through a door, Archie followed her tug and let Sandra lead him to the drinks tray in the hall, where she poured him a stiff one.

Bottoms up, she said, encouragingly, and when Archie swigged: here's to 1978, year of the nursing home.

Bottoms up. Through the fancy fish-eyes in the bottom of the cut crystal, Archie saw briefly six Sandras, and he thought, the marvellous sameness of her! The neatness of her bob, still sharp and shining as the day they got married! The way she hadn't put on weight, when folk all about them were thickening like Ayrshire cows! The way she was with Christine, so calm and cool, and never letting Archie spoil her – she was a wonderful mother, that was what, and a crying shame she couldn't have more. Sandra knew what she was about. She knew where to draw the line.

Cheers, said Archie to his wife, by way of expressing all this. Cheers. And he drank, and shook his head like a dog shaking off water, and smiled.

And Sandra said: And don't worry about Ruairi, old boy. It was years ago we went out. We were children.

But Archie wasn't thinking about that. If you'd asked him, he'd have said Ruairi never slept with her, he was almost sure of it.

The doorbell went: his boss and his wife, first guests, and Archie made them Dubonnet and bitter lemons, and showed them the French windows, and how the roll-out room divider worked. Then folks arrived in waves, and Archie was surfing them on a tide of bonhomie, saying, grand to see you, grand to see you, and aye, very smart, I gave Sandra a free hand with the colour, apparently it's *olive*. He poured any number of whiskies, and drank them too, and ate a hundred wee bits of oatcake and

haggis and salmon on rye. He chivvied along the girls
Sandra had hired to give out the canapés, and pinched
one of their bums. He got jolly with Christine and the
friend from Pollock Shields, showed them how to do the
Gay Gordons in the corner.

There were some irritations. Christine kept answering
the door. She was wearing a wee flarey frock, peasant
style, and she swished it, and she tossed back her long
red hair, and said, come on through to the lounge, in a
way that spooked Archie for some reason, but you could
hardly stop her. The Dubonnet ran out, and the ginger
ale. His sister Fiona refused to fetch his mother to the
party. She said that Archie had made his bed now, and
bought the whole package, and done a deal, and he
should live in it, lie in it, whatever, and their mother had
always hated her and she was going to have a drink.
After that, the image of the old lady laid out on her high
bed flashed up in Archie's mind from time to time, bright
as a museum exhibit in the directional spotlights, and he
worried each time that she had never got the hang of the
spotlight switches, wouldn't be able to turn them off for
a sleep, wouldn't be able to close her poor old eyes.

And of course there was Ruairi, constantly in the
periphery of his vision, next to the Christmas tree, by
the drinks table, hanging off the doorframe, looking like
Rob fucking Roy in a crumpled white shirt and his old
school kilt. Ruairi smiling his long slit of a smile, pushing the wing of his hair – still black – out of his narrow

dark eyes with his thin, knuckly hand; talking to Catriona, the very same Catriona of the letters whose heart he had broken enough times by now, surely.

It's all right, said a girl's voice by his side, he'll be good.

Archie turned. There was a young girl standing there. She had one of those hairdos with the curls all turned under. She said: You're Archie. I'm Colette, Ruairi's girlfriend.

A page boy, that was what the do was called. And a Catholic name. And a Glasgow voice. She didn't fit here, and she didn't look much like Ruairi's type, however young she was. She was dark, she was wearing a trouser suit, she had glasses, and she had a glint in her eye. Clever. Ruairi didn't like them clever. Jenny was blonde, and dumb as a sheep.

His wife's here, said Archie.

His ex-wife, said the page boy. It's all right. Jenny and I are quite well acquainted. And looking at the group again, Archie saw that Jenny was right there, looking hellish in a high-necked frock, dressed ham in a frill. Ruairi had one of his children by the armpits, wee Andrew, and was tossing him up, whirling him round. The dark had come out in the child, all right. You could think he was Pakistani.

Ruairi said, said the girl, that you might be a bit awkward with it all. So I thought I'd reassure you.

Aye, said Archie, I see.

I met Ruairi at work, said the girl. I'm actually at Alan and Cartwright? I'm a secretary.

A modern miss, said Archie. He thought she was a grammar school girl, doing nicely for herself.

And Ruairi, said the girl, works there in an assistant capacity to Mr Cartwright.

Pushing the wheelchair? said Archie. Al Cartwright was his grandfather's last friend. He must be a hundred.

But, said Colette, not for long. I'm not having it. I said to him, go back to your music. Back on the road. Life's too short.

Back with the wee jazz band? asked Archie. Not that he knew anything about it. He'd never been to see Ruairi's band. Not even the time they played City Hall.

Colette said: No, this is more like folk. Fusion? And he's the singer now. Trumpeter to singer. Like Louis Armstrong.

Archie didn't know who that was. He reckoned Colette must play herself.

I play the fiddle, said Colette. And the whistle. But for the band, I'm mostly managing. That's what the boys need most.

Now that she was smiling, Archie could see that he'd been wrong about Colette: she was very pretty. Her skin was very white, and she had dimples. And something else: she looked like his dead Aunt Flora. That quick, eager birdiness, the shining eyes.

He said: Is Ruairi really up to all that? I mean, all the weddings and the wee pubs? It used to get him down.

That took off her smile for a minute. But then she put it back on. She said: Archie, Ruairi wants you to know there are no hard feelings on his part about the house. None at all.

No hard feelings? said Archie. He thought: what would a girl like that know about houses? Grew up in one room in a tenement.

No, said Colette, really not.

Listen, said Archie. Listen. This was never his house. It's my house. This was left to my mother, and to me. He was suddenly aware he was right up against the girl, cornering her. Are you clear? he said, and he could feel her breath on his neck. She looked actually frightened.

Archie, said Sandra from behind him. And Archie breathed out, and turned, and leaned back on the party, and the party inflated under him and carried him away, but whatever he did after that, even when he was dancing Strip the Willow and swinging a scarlet Christine like a niblick in a bunker, he kept glimpsing the girl Colette's shiny hair, talking to Catriona, talking to the wee friend from Pollock Shields, and he knew in his heart that at some point she would get Ruairi to do his singing.

And so, when, soon enough, Catriona came sashaying across the carpet to pick the needle off the record, and Colette produced a violin case and opened it, Archie was at least prepared. He rushed into the kitchen, swinging the swing doors and saying *Phew!* in the manner of a screwball comedy, to make the whole thing seem a bit of a jape, appropriate to the season. But the hired girls carried on washing up at the sink, and the piper, a short fat teenager with a heavy blond face and a bright blue kilt, carried on screwing on the pipes to the belly of the bag.

Had he ceased to exist? From the next room, the violin made some rosined, effective soundings, and a child squealed, and before you knew it Ruairi was singing 'My Love She's But a Lassie Yet'. The piper looked up. He's awful good, he said.

We're going to play a wee joke, said Archie.

The piper stared at him, his bottom lip hanging pink and loose. A joke? he said.

Aye, said Archie, you're going to go in there and play 'Amazing Grace'. Kid on like you can't hear him. The singer. D'ye ken what I mean?

The piper didn't seem to. He gazed, peebly. He said, it wasnae midnight for another five minutes.

So? said Archie.

The piper licked that loose lower lip. The noise of applause filled the kitchen. The girls had stopped washing up, and were staring. It just isnae the kind of thing I do, he said.

Next door, the violin made a few deep sweeps and Ruairi started again. Black treacle, hushed silence. 'John Anderson, My Jo': the very worst song in the world.

Archie reached into his sporran and found the fiver he had tucked there in case, last time he took Sandra to the Hunt Ball.

I want you, he said to the boy, to pipe in the black bun.

The black bun? said the teenager.

Aye, said Archie. Now.

And so the boy took the money and started up that terrible wheezing hovercraft business on the pipes, and Archie picked up the black bun and a great big knife from the kitchen and walked behind the piper into the dining room, into the song, with a kid-on march, like it was pre-planned, like it was a tradition.

It worked a treat. Folk laughed and cheered, and when Archie put the platter down, the boss said that it was wonderful, wonderful, and Archie picked up the knife to do the cutting, and Sandra said, Wait up, I'll come and help you, and the two of them were standing there, cutting the bun, like a wedding, and Archie was tuning the radio so the chimes would come at midnight and music with it and no fucking chance of Ruairi doing 'Auld Lang Syne' when the noise came from the door, and at first Archie thought, could it be the fog horns from the Clyde, already? But it was his mother.

Grace was wearing her nightie, on backwards, and Archie's purple jacket, which he had left, he recollected, in her bathroom. It gave her a forlorn, Victorian air, so that with her hand upraised she looked like nothing so much as the ghost of Christmas Past, gazing round at the baffled crowd and wailing with her mouth open, round and empty of all teeth.

Then she stopped. In the quiet, Ruairi walked forward and took her hand.

Grace, he said and she smiled at him, quite confidently.

I know you, she said, in her old, old, voice. I know you, darlin'.

Ruairi looked down at her with his long smile and his liquid black eyes like a deer's. Of course, he said, Grace. Of course you know me.

Ay, she said, you're my wee dark gentleman. I knew you'd be along.

And Ruairi tucked her old hand into his shirt-sleeved arm, and stroked it.

Come on now, Grace, he said.

So he walked her, in her long whites, down the aisle of green carpet the piper had formed, towards Archie and the bun. From the radio came the grave chimes of the New Year, but still no one moved towards each other, no one spoke, as if that pair walking forward in their quaint clothes had stopped each heart as they passed, as if their path was a path of frost. And it seemed to Archie, standing with the knife, that each one they touched was turned into his enemy; that he too had always known his cousin Ruairi for what he was; that he strewed ashes from his hands.

# The Invention of Scotland

It was the seventies; it was the Bay City Rollers; it was
Margo MacDonald; it was all our oil. A low purple cloud
rolled over Scotland, weeping Gaelic forenames, and
when it had passed, girls were mostly called Fiona. Come
the eighties, there were four in my Higher English class,
*Fiona Beaton and Fiona Seaton and Fiona Carmichael and
me*, as Mr Duncan sang, handing back our essays on Evil
and Macbeth.

Fiona Beaton was really called Beaton, and she was
my friend, but the other two were not Seaton or Carmichael, that was an old song. Though indeed, why not
confuse us? What a muchness we were, what a bunch
of callowness and freckles and half-open mouths! Here
I am, thirty years on, rattling in the toffee-jar of memory
for the real names of those Fionas, and find nothing in
my palm but the name McGarrigle, and no singular face,
no particular pair of hockey-playing calves, unwrapped
by those crackling consonants, either.

Ophelia Blane-Huntingdon, though, I remember.

Surely, we all do, Fionas Seaton, Beaton, and Perhaps-McGarrigle. She bore such a curious name, after all, and she arrived a week late into the term, and – oh scandalous origin! – from London, England. And then she was so thin and so beige all over; and her long legs ended in such outlandish heels; and her books were tossed in such a flimsy straw bag! It was as if a camel had walked into our classroom and folded its legs on the flip-top desk; as if such a flagrantly inappropriate, long-lashed desert creature had said to our beloved greasy-eyed old teacher in his knitted tie: I did read the Grassic Gibbon, Mr Duncan, but I found it – well, a little *Cold Comfort Farm*, to be honest. I mean, didn't you? All that stuff with the spurtle?

Mr Duncan's aquiline feathered eyebrows shot up, he flushed, but he grinned, despite the cheek to Grassic Gibbon whom he worshipped as a god. Fiona Beaton tutted, but when I turned across the aisle to Calum MacAlastair, I saw he too was sitting up, and his hands had dropped under the desk to the region of his spurtle, and he was staring at Ophelia's strange transparent greeny eyes through his own, famously black and sulky, peepers. And I saw then that Ophelia Blane-Huntingdon knew a thing, a thing I did not, and I made up my mind that I, who was a powerful and assured person within the confines of the school, who had already deputed for the leader of the debate team, would, whatever the opinions of Fiona B, befriend this frail piece of exotica, and that in return for my protection and condescension, she would show me how to make Calum MacAlastair mine.

And so it happened that after a few coffees in Morningside; after a trip to Rose Street where Ophelia refused to join in our preferred activity of hanging one another up from the crotch of our prospective jeans and closing the zip by main force, and instead daintily buttoned up and purchased Edinburgh's first pair of 501s; and following an exotic excursion led by Ophelia into what were then the unimproved pawn shops and stinking old clothes stalls of Stockbridge: I was invited – you may as well come in, I think she said – to Ophelia's flat in Royal Circus, and met her mother, Clarissa.

Clarissa was the first adult I ever called by her first name, or who wore jeans, or who was divorced. She had her hair tied up in a handkerchief like Mrs Tittlemouse, and she had a tiny, cheekbony, retroussé face, like a cat's, and pale lipstick on her scornful long mouth. You girls will have to cook, she said, that day. I've a deadline and a post to catch.

*Clack clack* went the typewriter, and we went through to the kitchen. It was a high, stone, Georgian room with an astragalled window and a window seat, the very sort I have recently paid a fair fortune for, but all I saw then was the mess: the cracked jammy plates dumped on the scarred wood table; the sheets drooping from the pulley to the ash-tray; the pots with boiled-over stew on the stove. *Slum!* said my mother in my head, for her kitchen was newly fitted with some of the first wipe-down fake-wood in Corstorphine, and her days were spent at war with germs.

Where's the cloth! I burst out, gagging, but Ophelia merely shrugged her shoulders and sat on the window seat, took up her cigarette, and lit it.

Ma should be getting on with her novel, she said, not rushing stuff out for the Sundays.

It took me a minute to realize the Sundays were the newspapers, and I thought it would be grand, to write for them, but I thought of *The Railway Children*, and quickly said: Oh but she has to keep a roof over your head.

Ophelia raised her eyes to the pulley and puffed on the fag. And she's been ill, she said, did you know? Cancer.

No one said that word aloud then, cancer – my mother used to draw a 'C' in the air with one finger – and I found I was unable to reply. Then Clarissa came in, shaking her manuscript like a wet towel.

Ophelia, she said, I'm out of envelopes. You'll have to run to the post office and buy one and send this by guaranteed.

She'll be too late, I said, glancing at my watch.

She'll simply have to shoulder the door open! said Clarissa, smiling, and Ophelia went out. Now, said Clarissa, I hope you're admiring my kitchen, Fiona?

I thought she was joking. I said: Are you having it done? And Clarissa, not replying, but talking all the while in her low, resonant purr, showed me all the things she loved about the kitchen: the original dresser with its high narrow shelves, the Edinburgh press with its deep ones, the eighteenth-century glass in the window, the slate-shelved larder and the wire-netting meat safe which swung out of its window, and how she had *exposed*, *stripped*, *sanded*, even *distressed* these *features*, so they looked older, not newer. As she talked, she tidied, very effectively, till all the dishes were in the (butler's) sink.

But this little bit of modernity, said Clarissa, I did insist on. And she picked up a shower head, small and silvered, specially plumbed into its own little tap, and used it to sluice the rubbish from the plates. Edinburgh's fugitive sun lit up the great window, and I saw the hand-blown curve on the window-glass, and the gilt on the chipped plates, and my heart bubbled with admiration like Clarissa's round-bellied jug, filled to the brim under the high brass tap. That was another thing: in my house, we always put a pot of tea on the dinner table.

After that, I went to the flat in Royal Circus most days, on my way back from school. Clarissa was still, as Ophelia said to me, as I said to my mother (making that 'C' sign in the sky, moving my hands down my chest, nodding), getting over an 'operation', and she found the stairs hard, so I helped Ophelia shop and carry the messages up from Stockbridge, and took articles to the post, and documents to be faxed from a basement in Hanover Street.

I learned: Ophelia was especially clever and going to be famous. From the chaise longue, Clarissa told us the stories. How, when she got to Oxford, Ophelia would act, or edit the magazine, or be President of the Union. How she would go to the ball. It would be Christchurch Ophelia would go to, or Univ, not a woman's college: Ophelia told me this herself, on our way to the bus stop. One day, when we were doing Careers, I even got the prospectus for Oxford down from the high shelf myself, and wondered how clever I was, and if my parents, who were already appearing to me differently, as pallid, provincial persons, like Leonard Bast, could afford the thing called Seventh Term.

Ophelia had to keep up her studies: she'd had a knock, said Clarissa, adjusting to the Scottish system. So I lent her my notes, which were colour coded and highly detailed and in ring binders, and sometimes, after school, if Ophelia wanted to study in the Chambers Street library, I would go on my own to the flat, and clear the kitchen and empty the washing machine and hang the towels on the pulley while Clarissa sat at the kitchen table and talked in that deep, low, even voice about all sorts: her divorce, for instance; and money and the 'hellish' lack of it; or 'the best things' to be seen in Florence or Rome; or the invention of Scotland in the nineteenth century and what a lot Walter Scott had to answer for, and Balmoral and Queen Victoria, of course, but mostly the Prince Regent in his kilt and pink tights. Once, she told me that Fiona was a phoney name, a Latin feminine stuck on a Gaelic word by a poet called Macpherson, and so enchanted was I that I felt only a skelf of shame. She lent me books: paperbacks from the towering shelves in the drawing room, E. M. Forster, Evelyn Waugh. She asked me about them when I'd read them, and drawled her praise of my 'incisiveness', and my 'terrific backbone'. She showed me what anchovies were, and how to make leaf tea. I still remember.

Her own backbone did not seem to be terrific. As winter set in, there was less talk of deadlines, less clack from the typewriter, and Clarissa was more and more often already on the chaise longue when we came in, clutching a rug with her little claw hands. Oh, Mummy, Ophelia would say, getting under the rug at the other end, it's so cold in this country, and Clarissa would throw up her hands and say: Darling Feely! But do look at the cornice! And I would make everyone tea in the large brown pot.

That's an awful lot of time you spend, said my mother, breathing hard as she paused in her vacuuming of the hall, with people who are not your family.

I knew she was right, and that there were balls I was dropping at home and at school that had taken me a long time to get in the air. But I was sold on the

Blane-Huntingdons, you see, sold as I am still sold sometimes when I enter a boutique where there is only one
of everything, and the price tags are handwritten, or
available only on application. In my mind, Clarissa was
writing prices on tags in her fine ink pen, and Ophelia
was tying them on my life with little silk ties, and looking at me with her see-through green eyes and daring me
to guess the numbers.

For Christmas, Ophelia gave me *The Pursuit of Love*,
and I gave her a perfume set from Boots, which I had
saved up for and knew was wrong. Clarissa gave me her
novel, her very own, a dry, thin paperback with an
etching of a punt on the front, epigraphed: 'To Fiona
who will come to great things'.

She underestimated the stairs, said my mother, bent
double as she cleaned the skirting boards with a tooth-
brush. That Mrs Blane-Huntingdon. When she bought
that flat.

Just Huntingdon, I said, Ms.

My mother nodded. She had dry, flaky skin and
whistle marks round her mouth, even then: I have inher-
ited the tendency.

And the winters, said my mother.

And the school. In January, Ophelia got Cs in her
mocks. I think Clarissa imagined, because there were
fees, that our school was a London school, that Ophelia
would lounge about in the sixth form, as they do in
England, and act in plays and lark in the library and call

teachers by their first names: but our school was nothing like that. It smelt of mud and formaldehyde; it echoed with the hammering keys of the Secretarial Studies Department and the animal cries of the rugby team; it was the size and style of a showpiece nineteenth-century factory. Like a factory, too, it was highly efficient: it chewed you in as a chapped and awkward twelve-year-old in a gym slip, and spat you out six years later as a prospective dentist. Ophelia, with her French French accent, her swooning over Ovid, her sneers for Grassic Gibbon and her cavalier essays, stuck in its metal maws like an exotic butterfly in the jaws of a Highland cow: she made it choke.

Besides, after the Cs, she largely gave up. She stopped studying in the Chambers Street library. She dropped Biology. She started to skive French. One day she said: Let's go to Jenner's after school, and I went, but in the perfume hall she stole two sample lipsticks from the display counter and put one in my bag. We got out and said goodbye, but when she had turned the corner, I threw the lipstick in the gutter, and when I got home I called Fiona B, said, come on, let's go to the Boys' Brigade concert, after all.

Nevertheless, that dark new year, that stillborn spring, I visited Clarissa. Twice a week, once a week, once a fortnight, taking the sheets to the laundry, dragging the coal from the hole. There was the day Clarissa said, I don't know what I would do without you Fiona, it is all so heavy. There was the day I saw Ophelia in Crawford's with Shona Dougie, who was famous for blow-jobs, smoking over a cappuccino, and walked on without saying hello. There was the day I knocked at the flat door and there was Ophelia, her uniform shirt half open, her thin skin flushed under it, and she'd ask me in but I'd be sure to wake Mummy up, and the grand door closed on me and I wept. And yet, and yet, the day Ophelia asked me for £76, because it was an emergency and only I would understand, I went to the Post Office and gave it to her. It was everything I had.

Your friend Ophelia, said my mother, bleaching the toilet, has gone to Gretna Green. With Eileen Mac-Alastair's boy. Him in your class. Calum. She raised her head to look at me. Did you know about that, Fiona?

I took it as cleanly as a weighing machine takes a penny, the pointer leaping silently round to *Overload*. I don't see much of Ophelia, these days, I said.

My mother nodded. That's what I told Eileen, she said. Poor woman's in some state. The amount they've paid, and Highers round the corner. She squiggled the brush round the bowl one last time, and flushed.

So I walked back to Royal Circus, back up the long stone stair. It was April: I brought daffodils. Clarissa answered the door, shrunk in a nightgown and shawl, no scarf on her head. Her hair was coming out in tufts; her scalp shone through, pearly. She took the flowers, and did not smile. How very yellow, she said.

In the kitchen, I set about gathering the dishes, putting them in the sink. You don't need to do that, she said, and I said I did, it looked like a bombsite. I'd put her novel on the table. She picked it up.

Are you giving it back? she asked.

I am, I said. It's not my sort of book.

The people in it swore so much, and were so thin, so London: it made me feel as if I were wearing fancy sunglasses, Ray-Bans such as Ophelia had and I did not, glasses that turned my family brown-green and old-fashioned as a cine-film. I knew I had to take them off.

No, said Clarissa. It's not for you.

It is thirty years. Around me, in my study, the shelves tower with books, all mine, in hardback, paperback and translation. Historical Fiction, under the name of Fiona Hamilton; Medical Love Tales by Fiona Dixon; Scottish Romance (a popular category, especially in the US) by Fionseach MacColl; and Crime, the Precipitous City series ('plots chewy and satisfying as Highland Toffee', *Scotsman*); published under my own name. No one reads Clarissa's book: it has not been republished, not even on Kindle. No one remembers, except me.

It's too English for me, I said. Mebbe.

No. You're too Scottish for it, said Clarissa.

I squirted a jammy plate with the little shower head. I placed it on the wooden rack above the sink. What's wrong with Scottish? I said.

Scotland, said Clarissa, is a province. I got it all wrong. I thought it was a country but it is not. Everything here is utterly provincial.

Thirty years. Houses in Edinburgh are no longer to be had for an English song, and I, I am so rich I have a whole one and a garden and have had the place done up by a decorator who specializes in vintage chic. My kitchen is hand built by craftsmen from Lewes; women in the Czech Republic have hand-stitched and then *distressed* my bedcovers; I have vast speckled mirrors ripped from a ballroom in France; even my paint comes from specialist pots named for country houses and I have paid extra for parts of it to be rubbed off. I should be over it by now: Clarissa's yellow-painted dish rack; Clarissa's window seat with patchwork cushions.

I put more hot water in the sink, started on the pans. Clarissa sat at the table and took a cigarette and lit it.

So, she said. Ophelia is in love.

Apparently so, I said, staring at the spermy gunk at the bottom of a porridge pot.

Is he a handsome boy? she asked.

Common-looking, I said.

Goodness, said Clarissa. How you do fancy him. Feely said so.

I breathed in, and my nose crackled. I imagined Feely, curled with her mother on the chaise longue, saying so.

Clarissa said: Of course, I told her to go. I said, love is love, whenever you find it. Life is for the young.

I felt she was lying. I said: He's stupid, but. She can wave bye-bye to university now. Oxford.

You are jealous, said Clarissa. Jealous because you yourself are so very dull. Dull and provincial and lower middle. And because no one loves you and you have postponed your life and will probably never have it. What are you doing here? Where is my daughter? And she started to cry.

And then I turned round from the sink, the shower head still in my hand, and it squirted on the floor, and made a wet bit on the boards. I thought, I should clear that up, and then instead I pushed towards Clarissa, and gave her a good squirt, all over her face and her robe.

She's a dirty wee bitch, I said. And she's left you.

She grabbed me, her nails sticking into my arm, and the water squirted everywhere. Then I gave her a shove, a proper one, and my blouse shed her claws as if they were no more than dried-out teasels brushing my coat on a winter walk. There she was, on the floor, a heap of washing, the showerhead beside her wetting her robe in dark stripes, a puddle growing. Slowly, her eyes all the time shut, she took her hands from her face.

Fiona, she said, and she opened one eye. Did I tell you, it's a phoney name?

You're wrong about that, I said.

I stooped and picked up the showerhead and dropped it in the sink and left it twitching like a snake with the force of the water. Then I walked out. I closed three doors behind me: the kitchen door, the flat door on to the stone stair, then the last one, the monstrous black one, twelve foot high, that put me back on the Edinburgh street.

I did not interrupt my studies to attend Clarissa's funeral, which was held a few weeks later in Hampshire: instead, I concentrated on my Highers and did well enough to skip the final year at school and go straight to St Andrews to study General Arts. From there I heard with satisfaction of the steady sinking of Ophelia Blane-Huntingdon: how she made the mistake, after her mother's death, of moving in with her new in-laws, and retaking Highers down at Broughton with her young husband, only of course to fail all her exams again and nearly kill poor Eileen MacAlastair with stress and split up with Calum and leave for London with her father. By the time I came to sleep with Calum MacAlastair myself – when he still had his eyes, before he lost his hair, but still no great shakes – she was said to be at the University of Sussex. Lately, I have heard on Facebook of her mediocre achievements in provincial television, and I have forgiven her.

Clarissa though, I do not forgive. She was wrong. It was a man named Sharp who invented Fiona, in the nineteenth century, and each one of us, each Fiona, has done plenty of inventing since. In my street alone there are four of us: Fiona Gill, who you will know from the television and who has a detached house with south-facing garden; Fiona James, an actuary married to another actuary with three children and half a house and half a garden and a nanny; and Fiona Stuart, a former actuary now a full-time mum married to an actuary who also has half a house and half a garden and no nanny. These last two half-houses, happily, do not adjoin. Then there is me: Fiona with the red hair; Fiona with the whole huge house and no child to put in it; Fiona who writes the books.

So many books, so many Fionas. How do you do it? asked a young journalist recently, and I told him my day. The early start, the fasting, the ten o'clock coffee. They like the homely detail. I showed him my yellow kitchen, my window seat, the cappuccino machine which grinds its own beans. Look, I said to him, here's money. And I showed him my butler's sink, and my sluice tap: its nifty silvered head, its long, retractable cord.

## Brunty Country

To be honest, Giles, I'd like a little more credit and a little less blame. I'd like you and the directors, and actually, the *whole firm* of Burns Pope Wilde, Literary Agents, to remember how and where this whole story started.

And that's in the slush pile, with me. No, I'm not complaining. I know it's where we all get our start! I'd just like you to recognize that I wasn't so much *in* it, as *on* it. I was sniffing it all over: yup, all of it, the lousy dog memoirs, the saddo comic novels, the picture books by perverts. I was using my nose the way a metal detector uses its bleeper in a prehistoric midden. My nose sniffed out the hand-bound, hand-sewn, loony booklet of *poems*. My nose said: Susannah, hold that one to the light.

Oh, I admit at first I thought I was looking at the world's best quill pen font. I was peering at the capitalization, trying to spot the repeats, when I noticed that I was also *reading* the poems. Maybe this guy Ellis Bell actually had something. The landscape, you know? All that death and snow and so forth? I was thinking: Teen Goth; Deep Green; Northern Soul — kinda Now. And then my nose was twitch, twitch, twitching, and I was reaching for my phone.

Of course there wasn't a number, not even a landline. And that's what I mean. Credit me, Giles: I didn't drop the case, I went there. I was on the train to Leeds before I noticed there wasn't a postcode.

Leeds was one thing, you can still shop; Hebden Bridge, also in the Starbucks Belt, nice interiors shops, you'd be surprised – but that place, H—? What can I tell you? It was off the map. It was off the satnav. Literally: the TomTom screen went blank. Brunty Country, said the taxi driver, drawing up in the lay-by, waving at a bit of moor. We don't go there any more. Not since what happened to Edgar.

I got out of the car. You know that noise when you're in the country? Those waves in your ears echoing, fading out? Like you've just been unplugged. Well, it gets on my nerves, to be honest, and I didn't know what to do. I'd come so far. I could see a road, though: grey dirt snaking through the grass. It's down there, you reckon? I asked the driver, but he was gone.

Well, I panicked, a bit, obviously. I tried my iPhone: no dice. That place was on – would you call it a ley line? Like no reception at all? Total cut-off? On the metalled road, you could get anything; I was face-timing Cara, getting her to double-check the name on an antique

Ordnance Survey. Two steps off it, a total blank. Even my compass utility wouldn't work. I thought about it carefully: I could hike back into Reception, call a cab, or I could walk down that road, into the Beyond. And I took Beyond, and I'd like you guys to ask yourselves, honestly, if you'd have done the same? Really? For a book of *poems*?

I'm not much of an outdoor girl, but I remembered it's important to keep hydrated, especially in extreme conditions, so after a mile or so, I stopped and broke out the San Pellegrino. I was in a *dell*, I guess. Sort of a dip, in a sunny bit? There was a stream running down a cliff, maybe six foot high, then it broadened out into a nice sort of brook affair. I mean, I suppose the water had to be polluted – it did foam on the waterfall – but it was clear in the stream. Brown and clear, like beer. So, if you can believe it, I took off my Converses, rolled up my skinnies, waded out to a nice flat stone in the middle, and sat there, cooling my ankles in the flowing Newcastle Brown. I even got out my Aviators and popped them on. It all looked better like that, in sepia. More natural.

The water burped and burbled, and I guess there are birds that sort of gurgle, too, but I know a laugh when I hear one. Something flicked in at the corner of my eye, something white, and I heard it again: a chilly, uppity, intellectually superior, snorty sort of giggle. I took off my glasses and I couldn't see anything. I put them on, and there she was, on the opposite rock. A five-foot figure in a Laura Ashley nightie, crouched on her haunches. Thick dark hair and a grey little goblin face with bushy eyebrows and this horrid, horrid, *quizzical* expression. Like what the fuck, townie, at me and my sunnies.

Well, I didn't run away. (Point for that please!) I said, Hi, I'm looking for Ellis Bell?

Ellis Bell, she said, grinning.

Yes, I said. You see, he sent me some poems—

He sent poems!

And I've come all the way from London to see about them.

From London, to see about them! she said, and, let me tell you, I had by this time noticed the repeating trick and was just a teensy bit off-put.

Do you know Ellis Bell's address? I said, and she stood up on her rock. You could see how thin she was through her nightie thing: muscly little monkey legs, and a horrible dark triangle at the crotch that I'm fairly sure was not a thong. Her feet were bare, gripping the rock like a hobbit.

Ellis Bell's address, she said, pointing down the road. I stood on my rock, followed the line of her arm. I saw a square grey house squatting *Psycho*-like on the horizon.

There? I said, quailing.

Air, she said, and when I turned, she wasn't there. And yeah, you could write it up as performance art, you can say she's super shy, and she's a fucking genius, but at the time, I was just spooked. Spooked and a little pissed off. I pulled my feet up onto the rock and started to dry them with my socks, and a little flat cloud went across the sun and turned the beauty off like a switch.

You look like a drain, I said to the stream, and it giggled at me, smugly. It took forever to get my socks on, and when I stood up, I couldn't see my way back, only forward, to the grey house, and still the wind was blowing through the grass like I was locked in a Wyeth Family landscape.

Air, Air, said a voice in my ear, and yeah, I got the fear. I split my Converses on that path. I lost my sunnies. I ran for the black door of the *Psycho*-house; the great brass knocker coming into focus like a lifebelt. I battered that door. I hung on to that knocker even when the door opened.

And who opened it? Not a corpse, which I was honestly by that time expecting. Not her nightyness, thank fuck, which had also crossed my mind. More Laura Ashley vintage weirdness, though. What I think about *that* is: it's a look, but it's actually quite a demanding one? You need a bit of height, shoulders, cheekbones, and *definitely* the daily Timotei, to carry it off, and the lady in front of me had none of these things. Her head came up, no kidding, to my bra, and her hair was, like, *embalmed* into a bun. But at least she smiled at me. Clever grey eyes in a pale little face. She said, Good day?

I'm looking for Ellis Bell, I said, and she actually clapped.

You're from the agency, she said. Thank God.

So there you are, you see. Next time you get started on the 'Susannah got off on the wrong foot with Charlotte' crap (no, you *do*. I've heard you at it), I'd like you to remember that little scene. Tiny, tough white hands, button cuffs, clapping. *Charlotte* clapping.

And what did I do next? Well, lots, actually. Lots of smiling. Lots of chatting. I coped fantastically, I'd say, considering I'd run over a moor and been scared half-witless by a lunatic. I was right in there, going gosh, gosh, what a super place, is that real limewash, I love the distressed look on the walls, is it genuine lamp-black? How do you do, Anne, and of course I understand that some people don't talk and prefer to sit by the fire and gibber. Gibbering is my favourite thing too!

Look, I sat right down in their lunatic low-carbon co-op kitchen. I said, super, a real stove! I ate the rock cake. When they pointed at the parlour door and went, shh shh, I shushed, like it was really super-normal to be scared stiff of your dad when you've got to be thirty-two. I whispered: And do you write yourself, Charlotte?, Poems! Lovely!, Belgium, what a fabulous theme! Could I have a look? Might I take it back to London with me, Charlotte?

A fine start with Charlotte. Do you take my point?

Look. I showed you *Professor*. You agreed with me:

change the gender; put in a hunky doctor; add a dead nun; and try for the Twilight Moms' market. You didn't say, put her on a retainer, cos otherwise she'll skip off to Hills Wilton with our sage advice in her pocket and that book'll win the Orange Prize and be on *Richard and Judy* too and keep us and one of our better publishers in funds for the next millennium. Or maybe I just didn't hear it.

The next bit, I admit, I didn't do so well. But I was set up. Picture this, OK? You're just about to say to Anne, who has come to sit beside you and is gently and a little spookily fingering your sweatshirt and murmuring about a hard life and something she's been writing; you're just thinking, *wow, do we have an abuse memoir here?*, when the kitchen door opens and in comes the Goblin of the Moor. You'd scream, right?

Well, I didn't, actually. I just said, Woo! Not, you scared the fuck out of me. Or, don't you think you should wear underwear with cheesecloth? Just: Woo!

Woo who! she said. Woo who London! And she started to dance round the room like a tiresome mime show in a cellar in Hoxton. She picked up this rock cake and made like it was a phone, waving it about. Reception, reception? And I'm thinking, *I get the feeling you're Ellis Bell, baby, and I'm losing faith in your* oeuvre, *big time*.

No, that's honest, and I stand by it. You see, when I go looking for writers, I'm looking for the package, not a screwball. You know? I want warm, handsome, presentable, telly friendly, non-abusive . . . I want Patrick Gale. Every time.

Oh really? Well, maybe it's a generational thing. Twenty years is a long time in this business, Giles, and, like, the Internet happened and all the old drunk pervy guys are dead and . . . Yes, I agree. Let's leave it there.

Where was I? Oh yes. Watching the Goblin dancing. Well, Charlotte gets embarrassed and she says: Susannah is an Agent, Emily. All the way from London.

An Agent of the Devil? says Emily, still dancing.

A Literary Agent, hisses Charlotte. Susannah, this is Ellis Bell.

I figured, I said. We actually met.

Emily flops into an armchair, stares at me, starts picking at her rock cake.

A literary agent, she says. And what is the book which sets your heart beating, Susannah? What is the literature that raises your doggish hackles? And she did a little dog mime, woof, woof.

Well, I say, very politely, I was awfully interested in Ellis Bell and his poems.

Emily waves the cake about her head. Do you want to bite them? she says. Do they inflame you? And, no kidding, she runs her hand down her nightie in this really inappropriately sexy way. Anne has her head in her little hands. Charlotte, though, is grinning.

Now, that *is* the point I fucked up. I know it. If I'd

given a different answer, right then, I could have left with the ms of *Wuthering* in my satchel. I'm sure of it. Cos, of course, Emily's interested in money and fame, really. A certain sort of fame. I think we've seen enough since the Booker to confirm that for us. Oh, come on: *the whole* of the *Observer* mag? The photo shoot on the moor? The collaboration with All Saints? Do you really call that Art?

OK. You do. Art. Should have mentioned it, shouldn't I? Susannah should have said, Yes, the poems inflame my heart with the truth of Great Art and make me sweat and salivate. But, as it happens, I didn't. I looked at the sneering goblin – yeah, she photographs nicely, but have you noticed, always in profile, mouth shut? No teeth, you heard it here first – and I said: No. I think you have a great font. Ever thought of developing an app?

Well, I was out before you could say Man Booker. She sort of clawed me, if you really want to know. And I squealed, and Charlotte and Anne went into this mime of terror cos of the noise, and Daddy and the Door, and – well, I just left. Closed the big black door. Outside, it had clouded over big time. In fact, there was a fog descending, thickest fog I've ever seen, wraiths of it, like dozens of Emilys in hundreds of nighties. I had another go at my compass utility.

Go on then, Giles, rage. Picture the Man Booker pouring through my hands like the fog. And then get over it, please. Because, if you ask me, Emily was looking at self-publishing from the start. She was already self-binding! I think she might even have already hiked over to Hebden before I visited. Hooked up with Claire at CliffTop Books. She was so damn quick off the mark, after all, wasn't she? Had it out a month after *Tenant*?

All right. I can understand you don't want to accept that. But here's another thought for you: maybe, just maybe, *WH* isn't really the eternal masterpiece we're all making out? Maybe it's just a small press novel that got really, really, lucky? You know, warm wind from Twilight, warmer one from Charlotte, the public in a hot mood for incest and cheap ebooks, judges all favouring the independent presses, Green stuff ensuring the good reviews? In a way, *WH* is very *fashionable*, you know? I mean, not as in iPhone, fashionable as in The New Portentousness? Like we live in the urban world and we all feel guilty as fuck so all we want to read about is moors and stones and pure feelings and all that tosh? And give it the flaming Booker.

OK, OK, a bit sour. Yup. We'll end it there. But I do want to leave you with this about Charlotte, at least. You've got to understand, Giles, she was always looking beyond Brunty Country. She wanted to be where the big shit happened. Look how quickly she'd moved to London. Moving through us was just a part of that: it really was not my fault. Besides, she has a thing for men. The way she fastened on to James at Hills Wilton is actually sort of scary. She wouldn't show me *Jane E*, would she? But James just had to dimple, and whoopy-doopy, she reaches in her nasty little hand-sewn underskirt pocket, and out comes the teen crossover classic. That relationship is *way* over-personal. Honestly. His wife's in fits, and there's nothing she can do, cos it's Charlotte pays the bills. Yup, that's Charlotte. Miss Nicey-Nicey with her rock cakes and her big grey eyes looking over my shoulder.

But I'm here to accentuate the positive. What I need now is for you, and the firm, to concentrate on Anne, and the future. Anne, bless her! It's no exaggeration to say I owe her my life. I was already half a mile off the path when she popped up beside me and took my arm. I was just yards from the boggy bit where Edgar the taxi driver drowned. I could have been a Seamus Heaney poem, easy as splish, splash, splosh. As it was, she walked me right out of Brunty Country, waited till the cab came, talked me through the whole story.

I gave her my iPhone, she gave me *Tenant*, that day. A nice day's shopping, in any other context. No, come on. *Tenant* got a major Betty Trask. Its sales are more than adequate. And she's segued into self-help just seamlessly. AA America is really interested in a tour. And it's Anne, let me remind you, who brought us this. The ms I've got on my desk right now. The one I really want some help with, Giles.

Hot? Giles, it's glowing. It's a rag-to-riches misery memoir that's going to be huge in the States, *plus* a parenting how-to book to out-sell Baby Mozart. How a boy from an incredibly humble background in Ireland escaped poverty, abuse and illiteracy to rub shoulders with the careless rich and excitingly pervy in Cambridge University. How he won and lost the love of his life. How he settled in the wilds of North Yorkshire and entered into a unique family experiment. How he raised not one, not two, not three, but four authentic geniuses! (Yup, we are counting Branwell. Tattoos were only ever a sideline. He's really in demand in Thrash Metal CD covers now. And he's cleaned up. Might even go with Anne on the tour.) Anyway. Just picture it. This is what we're all going to be reading this Christmas. I'm seeing monochrome cover, red indent lettering: *Patrick Brunty: My Story*.

And a subtitle.

Genius! How you can raise one too!

Because, in the end, Giles, isn't that what we all want to know? Not, I mean, not highbrow literary stuff. The Emily Romance. The Charlotte Art. No, the real stuff. The stuff we can apply to our actual lives. That's what Anne's got, and Patrick too, once you get past his super-scary nine-foot-tall mad-Irish persona. He's the centre of the action, remember, up in that house. His was the door that was closed, and now Burns Pope Wilde can open it! I'm seeing serial here, Giles, I'm seeing spin-offs, I'm seeing chat-show, I'm seeing *Oprah*. Trust me, Giles, it may have taken a few years to get here, but *this* is the real story.

# My Grandmother Meets
## Katherine Mansfield on the
## Packet from New Zealand
### in 1919

To get them all on the same boat, I have had to fiddle with things a good bit.

First, I had to drag my grandmother and my great-aunt Helen all the way from Christchurch on the South Island of New Zealand to Auckland on the North Island. They were not pleased. They had booked the packet from Christchurch. The war was over. They were on their way to England to start the lives they had been waiting for: to put Helen on the stage; to launch Virginia into independence; to reunite my great-grandmother with society and the turf.

So, didn't I think they had enough to do, already? Ordering their travel suits? Paying calls, exchanging cards, leaving addresses, poste restantes. Mending their best frocks from last year to be second-best next year?

Tucking their leather, their cotton, their kid gloves into pairs? Counting their silk stockings, best, less-best, everyday, grey, rose, rose, darned? Tucking the crackling tissue paper parcels into leather-edged compartments? Swinging those compartments into the body of a trunk? Locking the trunk? Labelling it? Saying goodbye, goodbye, they are never coming back?

Besides, the journey, by unsprung car and charabanc and small choppy steamer between the two islands, was frankly frightful. It always was: the New Zealand scrub is wilder, then, than we can imagine, the ocean vaster, the roads unmade. And the Cane girls are still less keen on the detour when they see Katherine Mansfield clambering on board the packet in Auckland Harbour. Her coat is half off her shoulders; her hair is standing up in great wisps round her head; her ivory-handled umbrella is thrust haphazardly through the leather straps of her bulging dressing case; she is late to start with and she quarrels to the last whistle with her vague, grand, beautiful mother and silly pretty sisters and handsome child of a brother, all of whom she leaves on the dock. Alone! To England, alone! What can she be thinking of? She has big eyes and a mean, small, gambler's mouth. She is not their sort.

Though the hair and the lateness is not entirely Katherine's fault, for once. In order to get her on board, I have had to drag her forwards through the briar brush of an entire eleven years, and even though she is used to being the oddball, the observer, not fully in the room, she is disconcerted. We will let her stand on the top deck a moment, smooth herself back into herself: not Katherine Mansfield at all, yet, but Kathleen Beauchamp, keeper of notebooks with not a lot in them, author of one ludicrous piece of juvenilia; the furious, ridiculous nineteen-year-old who left New Zealand in 1908. I've had to alter her clothes considerably – though, frankly, as she retains her plump, pre-TB figure, she should be pleased, the 1919 ones are more merciful. But Kathleen is never pleased. She fingers her serge skirt in disgust, tugs a big felt hat over the hopeless hair, scowls. She pulls out the ivory-handled umbrella from the trunk, and stares – I have removed it from a later story, and she does not recognize it – and looks about her, and sighs.

How tiny the boat is, really – and the harbour! But this is the past: they think it is large. Even Kathleen, who has been on the steam packet before, to school in London and back again, thinks so, and this boat is markedly more advanced than the last one she was on – though of course she will not say so. She tries to find a pose which indicates absolute indifference. My grandmother, who has soft brown hair and heavy eyebrows and a narrow, high-shouldered build, has no such ambition. She stands at the rail in her pale linen suit, and watches keenly as it all slips away: the low town glittering in the Antipodean light; and behind it, the wild green island she has lived on all her life. Kathleen lurks beside her, biting her glove-button, looking too.

One thing I have not made up: these two belong on the same deck. Decks are about class, and Kathleen and Virginia are of the same, highly specialized, tiny social group. All its members could get on the boat at a pinch: the children of the second and third generation of New Zealand English migrants who have built up successful businesses. My grandmother's family has the largest department store in the South Island. Kathleen's father has done even better: he is Chairman of the Bank.

They are a nervy, over-dressed, dreary lot: all distinctions faded when they left the old country, which meant they had to be reinstated with a vengeance as soon as anyone got the chance. Those who were least posh to start with – Kathleen's father – are the keenest snobs now: they imitate the ways of Surrey as best they can. The poshest – Kathleen's mother, my great-grandmother – can't bear anyone in New Zealand at all, and sigh for London. The Canes have a vast, vaguely Art Nouveau house called Pen-y-Bryn. The Beauchamps have a house in Auckland and another in a savagely beautiful part of the coast, which they have named, for God's sake, Chesney Wold.

Kathleen will be thirty, and fatally ill, when she returns in her mind to Chesney Wold to write *The Aloe*, *Prelude*, *At the Bay*; for my grandmother, it will be longer. She will settle in Benson, Oxfordshire, then

Winchester, Hampshire. She will make from her Irish, Catholic husband and his career as a Navy captain, mostly abroad, often in Russia, a life of astonishing Englishness, surrounded by chiming china clocks and objects of exquisite taste. She will take me to Stonehenge, St Catherine's Maze, the grave of Jane Austen. She will talk often of her time in Moscow, wife to the Naval Attaché – but of New Zealand, almost never. About the lamb chops sometimes, the earthquakes. She will tell me, just once, that *At the Bay* is a good story, the description is very like.

The island is almost gone now – a line in the far distance. Now there is only the boat, gallantly chugging over a vast ocean. Now there is only the deck and a brisk big wind and a handful of people held in by the rail and you would think the girls would at least exchange names in their matching, cut-glass accents – there is no such thing as a Kiwi voice, yet – names of the people they know in common, that handful of families who make up New Zealand Society. But already Kathleen is snubbing my grandmother, making it clear she thinks she is a little dull, with her Girl Scout enamelled badge pinned to her linen lapel, and her training in maternity nursing. Already, too, Kathleen has fastened on her target for the trip, the new, ravenous crush that will keep her going until she lands in Liverpool and starts hounding the life out of the unfortunate cellist Garnett Jowell: Helen, who is walking a little further up the deck, her small, starry head held elegantly high, the bullish, choleric Captain already at her side, pointing out something dreary about steam propulsion.

My grandmother observes this and does not care. Kathleen seems more than a little crazy; besides, Virginia is never resentful of her glamorous younger sister. She does not mind that Helen is the reason for this trip; nor that Helen has the softly drawn-together eyebrows and pearly skin and wide eyes and air of demure, wounded sensuality that is perfectly 1920, perfectly Clara Bow. She will not mind, later, that Helen shares the play bill with Edith Evans, or marries a very rich admirer and, when she is widowed, his brother. The sisters will stay close all their lives, bring up their children together, bear each other's losses. When, fifty years from now, Helen lives in a stupendous vicarage in Hampshire with Saki the Pekinese, Charles the cook, and a kitchen-garden the size of my childhood, and Virginia has a very modest retirement flat in Winchester, she will not resent that either, but will visit every week. They will sit together in Helen's green and white drawing room, quietly at one, as they sit now at supper, letting Kathleen make wilder and wilder conversational stabs at the great smooth dullness of the Captain's table.

Whizz! Up go her bright remarks like little fireworks: she thinks sunsets at sea are like a bed, with great squashy cloud pillows, and she wants to just roll on them! Does Helen ever feel like simply ripping her clothes off and leaping overboard? Helen receives each remark with one eyebrow raised. She gives a neutral nod. She lets the notions drown like wasps in cream. Kathleen is frustrated. Generally, she is as rapacious, domineering and successful with girls (the Maori princess, golly! The unfortunate Ida Baker, gosh!) as she is clumsy, obvious, and downright ludicrous with men. She turns to the Captain, who prides himself on his close relationships with the upper deck, especially the young ladies.

The Captain leans back in his chair, touches the waxy ends of his ginger moustache. He has news. In a few days, they will cross The Line. The equator, he means, but they all know this, are well prepared for the famous shenanigans that take place there. A party, says the Captain, and some dunking, but nothing excessive or crude, and what would the young ladies think of taking part in the masque? He will be Neptune, and carry a trident.

My grandmother is glancing round, checking that her mother is not included: such things have been known to happen. Helen is smiling politely, wondering exactly what she will be required to sing. Kathleen is caught between utterly despising everyone and the ritual, and wanting desperately to be included. The Captain says he will need a queen. He has his eye on Helen, of course. He is thinking of buckets of water, transparent linen, prongs, but Kathleen galumphs in and says she will write something for it, something new, and somehow no one stops her.

Which is how it comes about that Helen, instead of being Queen Amphitrite and presiding over a little mild dunking on the top deck while wearing a green wig, finds herself singing a 'Lament for the Drowned' (original composition, K. Beauchamp), to Kathleen's accompaniment. It is noon, and the sun is direct as a gunshot. The wind carries away almost all sound. It is entirely unsuitable and unwanted, and Helen knows it. Only pantomime will do here, only the round-mouthed shouts of the captain, the cheers of the crew, who have assembled, leathery and cordy and unfamiliar, to have a bit of fun, a rest in all this heat, not stare at one girl in white opening and closing her mouth while another girl in green silk two sizes too small saws away on a cello.

Besides, it is almost impossible to play the cello on any kind of steam packet and this one is currently mounting waves on a scale with burial mounds in Hampshire. The engine splutters and drags and, however hard Kathleen squats over the instrument, she cannot keep its metal post secure on the decking, and just as the piece reaches its climax and Helen sounds the three high whoops (stormy petrels) required of her, the cello flips up on its stalk, and Kathleen follows it, upturning her three-legged stool. Her advanced, modern, greenstone necklace catches in the neck of the instrument and bursts, and its beads roll all over the deck, and she sprawls after them, her dress riding up, showing the darns in her right stocking.

Ha, Ha, Ha, Ha! laughs Neptune, striding forward in his seaweed beard. Kathleen sits up, smoothes her skirt down. Ha, Ha, Ha! laughs the crew, laugh the passengers, laughs Helen with her head thrown back. Ha, Ha! laughs Kathleen and she gets to her knees and decides to leave the beads. Neptune turns kindly away, hands Helen her gold paper crown, her trident made of tin and oyster shells. Now she is Queen Amphitrite, conductress of guffaws. She will ascend the throne.

A steward offers Kathleen a sunburnt hand, then a winceyette arm, and she pulls herself to her feet. She glimpses my grandmother pacing the deck, stooping to the ground like a kiwi, and wonders what she is doing. The steward picks up the unfortunate cello by the neck and walks it into the lounge. Kathleen follows and sits on a green leather chair by a card table. The steward brings a glass of water. The glass door shuts, and the noise of the wind is quietened. Kathleen sips the water, shuts her eyes, and hates them all, very much.

The door clicks. It is my grandmother. She comes to Kathleen's side, sits, opens up her handkerchief. She has gathered up the jade and jet beads of the wrecked necklace. Carefully, she opens a card box which is stored on the table, takes out the neatly tied bridge set, pours the beads into the green baize interior. Do you have the chain? she asks, and Kathleen, who has been chewing it, hands it to her mutely. My grandmother starts to re-string the beads: one big green bead, two black, one green. She has a plan for the shattered clasp.

All her life, my grandmother will sew and mend. We have her roll-up needlework set still, hand-embroidered, pink and green. A holder for the thimble and a loop for scissors, a book for the needles, a pocket for the sewing plaits, a pouch for scraps. She made it herself, for travel. She will show me how to start a seam properly, and finish one, and how to darn, and I will not learn. My grandmother will say to my mother: how can a woman work? She must care for her children and then her parents. My mother will not be offended. She will keep the sewing set. She thinks my grandmother wasn't right, but had a point. So do I.

Kathleen is not offended by the mending now: she is soothed. It makes her think of her own, blissfully unjudgemental grandmother, the one who did the work. She says to Virginia: you have beautiful hands.

Long hands, says Virginia. People say, I should play the piano. But I can't. She smiles. (When I grow these hands myself, and encounter the same problem, she will say this to me.) Or paint, she goes on. I can't do that either.

But her father can, rather good watercolours, and her grandfather did, some of the first records of Auckland, and her beautiful daughter Elizabeth who died when I was seventeen will paint too, and Helen's daughter

Sarah, and Elizabeth's son Matthew will make vast strange sculptures in the Chinese desert. All her life, Virginia will press flowers, polish pebbles, arrange rooms like Dutch paintings. Paint? I think she must have decided not to.

Outside, on deck, Helen is crowned with gold paper. The Captain is scarlet with lust and sunburn. Kathleen doesn't care. She is glimpsing the best of my grandmother, the clarity of vision, the austere, intelligent kindness that goes with it. She leans forward: What do you like? she asks. What do you do?

And now, now, they could actually have a conversation. My grandmother could tell her about the life she has chosen. About her nursing training. The babies, and what you do with them, and Dr Truby King with whom she had been studying. And Kathleen might drop the many layers of affectation with which she has necessarily covered herself, with which she is inventing herself, and actually tell Virginia about the Trowell boy, and her other awful passions and reckless experiments, and Virginia, intuiting things she could never ask, might quietly tell Kathleen, one day while they are pacing round the deck, not looking at each other, a few things she has learned in her training, while spending so very much time with wombs, with access to the whole of Christchurch University Library. And Kathleen could listen and pick up a few basic hints about how to avoid pregnancy, and even where and how to obtain an early pessary, and could thus avoid that miscarriage in Germany, and the consequent sterility, and maybe even the gonorrhoea which will combine with the TB to finish her off at the age of thirty-five.

But already the boat I have so poorly sewn together, have constructed in fact from two different black-and-white diagrams, is splitting down its ill-assorted seams, and the internal stairs are languishing like loose springs into the waves, and down the scrubbed decks and into the desperate depths slides the girl Kathleen. Down to meet Katherine Mansfield, thin and tragic author of 'The Garden Party', and that oddball John Middleton Murry, and her handsome brother Leslie in his army uniform. Dear Chummie, Kathleen loved him so much, so much, she remembered it when he was dead in a trench.

And down, down, into the ocean, go all the silly stuffed passengers, turning as they slide into spats and beads, shoe trees and coat stands, the contents of a pawn shop in Stockbridge, a copy of *The Enchanted Castle*. Down goes the cello, and the piano, and the card box of beads, and the greenstone necklace, and my grandmother's spillikins and her lamb chops and her polished pebbles and her pictures made of wild flowers, and my great-aunt's meringues and fruit cages and their mother's china statue of the Blue Boy, and this great journey which my grandmother never mentioned, not to me, not really, and Time, disguised as the sea, swallows them all. Soon there will be nothing but the great green waves heaving up and down, far from any shore, and, bobbing on the top, a single copy of *Bliss and Other Stories*, tough and small and unsinkable as a black-headed gull.

# The Book Instead

Me and Rachana are in her room, we are doing our English. The title is *The View From My Window* but Rachana's view isn't much: just the tar paper roof of the extension then the garden then rubbish then the train tracks, shimmering, and that is only fifty words, even with 'shimmering' put in at the end. We are waiting for a train to pass so we can put that in too, when Rachana says let's write a book instead, and I say, OK.

You be the writer, says Rachana. You're good at English. You can use my pen with the pink fluffy top. This book will be a bestseller maybe, maybe they will make a film.

I take up the pen. I get a new piece of paper. I say, OK, what will the book be about?

Rachana says, about some friends. About girls our age. Like in a good book, like in books about Mary-Kate and Ashley. About girls like us.

Rachana is my age and my shape and my cousin. We

are short fat Indian girls in West Ham shirts, and we are not in books.

The girls go on a picnic, Rachana says. They are on summer camp and they have a canoe.

They have an accident, I say.

Yes, says Rachana, and maybe someone dies. Not the main girl but her friend maybe.

What is the main girl called? I say.

Patricia, says Rachana. Trixie for short. And I think this is a stupid name but I don't say so yet.

Are there boys in the story? I say.

Yes, says Rachana, there is a boy, his name is Rafe, he drives the rescue canoe.

Listen, I say, *Rafe's hair lies thickly on the collar of his polo shirt*. Because now I am writing. Now the fluff on the pen bobs across the page like a rabbit and outside a train roars and passes. *Rafe's hair falls over his face and he pushes it back with a slim tanned hand* . . .

Rachana says *and he smiles, showing perfect teeth*, and I write it down.

Can we say about his chest, I say, where his shirt comes down, you know, in a vee, at the bottom, sometimes you see a boy's chest, but Rachana says that's rude.

OK, I say, I'm writing more about his hair, I'm writing *it's jet black with a sapphire gleam*.

No, says Rachana, Rafe is blond.

How can he be blond if he is Indian? I say.

He's American, says Rachana.

Some Americans are Indian, I say. Lots of them are. Uncle Saleem and all the cousins, they're American Indian?

That sounds funny, says Rachana. And anyway in stories the main boy is English, English American. Let's write about the canoe.

Why, I say. Why is it a summer camp? Why is it America?

Because stories are in America, says Rachana.

But I have the pen. I write: *Rafe pushed back his lustrous black hair from his tanned forehead, and smiled.* I write: *Samir had seen a beautiful girl, her lustrous black hair bounced on her shoulders with a sapphire gleam, she had a gorgeous voluptuous figure under her West Ham shirt she was thirteen years old her name was Rama.*

You can't put yourself in a book says Rachana, that is all wrong.

But I say, look, I just did.

# This Problem Is For You

I shouldn't be here. The Unit's for loonies, for thickos, for weirdos, for kids that don't talk. Anorexic. Self-harming. Selectively Mute. I don't belong here, just because of what happened. I've told them to sort it. Told them I ain't staying. Ashleen, thirteen. No, don't write it down.

*I am this boy who does not speak. I am Samuel Kuffor. I am not always here. I am born in Africa. When I am two years old my mother left me with my grandmother and after ten years she came back, and she said we can go now. At the airport, they look at my passport for a long time, so long, I lean on the white cold counter and rest there. When they say, OK, you go now, I raise my head and the white comes too, like chewing gum, like biting your mosquito net in the night. That is where the white comes from, the white in this country, the white over the sun. That is why I am always cold.*

I'm not going to talk to you. You want to talk? Talk

to yourself. Talk to the hand. Look. Hand is talking, out of the hole of my fingers and thumb. I've coloured it black. Hand's got nice fangs. I drew them on with a pen. Talented aren't I? Gorgeous as well. Do you like my hair? Purple, I dyed it. Like Perrie Edwards. Don't you like it? Do you think I care? Hand likes my hair. Hand says hello. Say hello, Ashleen's hole.

*My mother say, in England you have opportunity for school, but in my country too I went to school. I was good at school I was Maths champion. We had a board, and the teacher scratched the problem, white on black, and call: Samuel Kuffor, this problem is for you! I look in my head and there is the answer, a pot on a shelf, and I take it down. Here, in Maths, I see the question and I know it is easy, it is junior-boy question, but when I look in my mind, the shelves are all empty. The board is electric, here. None of the answers stay.*

Just henna. Ain't permanent, and they can't tell me to wash it, cos that's racist, ennit? Cos they don't tell the Pakis, when they do it for Eid. No, ain't racist to say that. I ain't racist, Saira's my friend. She wrote *Islam* in Arabic, there, back of my hand. Do you like the writing? Arabic, ain't it. For my birthday, I'm gonna get a tattoo. Inking. Cher Lloyd. Yeah, I know I'm too young. They don't always ask you. Don't you believe me? I've got one already. A secret, can't show you. A personal place. *That's what makes you beautiful*. That's what my tattoo's gonna say. In Arabic writing. Right here, on my arm.

I said to Saira, I like that *Islam*, gonna get that tattooed on my hand, and she's like, tattoos are haram. *Haram*, that's forbidden. I'm a white girl, *Haram*, but they still fancy you, Pakis. Pakistani. I didn't say it nasty. It's true, they like the blonde girls. I used to be blonde, but I cut it all off. No, I'm not a Muslim, or Christian. I'm normal. I'm English. Some Muslims are normal, they even do Christmas. My boyfriend, he's Muslim, but normal like that. Albanian. They got Muslims there.

*In this country my mother works in the night and the morning in the hospital. She leaves my clothes on the chair, washed, ironed, everyday a white shirt, she leaves my bus money. Every Monday, I must go School Office for lunch tickets. My mother comes with me the first time, but the second time she works and I go myself.*

*Then there is a problem, and that problem is, you must sell your lunch ticket. The lunch ticket say £2.50, but you must sell it to the boys for £1. One boy explain this to me, Albanian boy. Is so you can choose to spend your money, he say, so you have freedom to not buy lunch, buy other things, but I want to choose lunch, £2.50, veg option, because if my mother work double shift, there is no dinner at home until 10 p.m. So when my Tutor have a Fortnightly Conference with me, One-to-One Mentor, I say about the lunch, I prefer to keep the ticket, please can I, and Miss Connolly close her mouth and say OK, and the next Monday I collect the tickets no problem and for three days I eat the lunch and it is all OK.*

*Then I am going home and the Albanian boy stop me. Africa, he say. Hey Africa, you are black, black boy, look you are black as my shoe, hey, you polished boy, what country you come from eh? Must be nice and hot. And he smile and he put his arm round me nicey, nicey, and he explain that I have made a mistake, and it is not my fault because in Africa they have mistakes. He say that here there is a rule that you do not say his name. I have broken this rule, so now I will give the lunch tickets, and because he is kind, the money will be 50p, and also I must give him my locker key. He is smoking cigarette. He say: If you say my name, your mother will die, like this. And he blows out a ring of smoke, and sucks it back in and eats it.*

Have you got a boyfriend? Does he love you? How do you know? Does he give you good stuff? My boyfriend he give me a laptop. And a balloon. A foil one, for my birthday. Is he handsome, your boyfriend? You got a photo? I'll show you mine.

Handsome. He's gorgeous. He's right good at football. Mediterranean complexion, *olive*, found that out from a quiz. He give me five perfumes, designer, in bottles. I writ him a poem. He took me to the cinema. Took me to the fair. You jealous much? That's real love, ennit? When you're still young?

What they said wasn't true. All he was doing was, like, looking out for people, like kids in this school? He looked out for the little kids, the soft ones, the ones fresh from Heathrow. You don't know what he did. He never hurt anyone. You don't know those people. He took some shit.

He give me a phone. Look, it's better than yours. Do you want to see my poem? I writ it. I writ: *I used to be nothing, now I am something.* I writ, *I love how you run, like the wind in the grass.*

*So after this day, I walk to school: forty minutes. I look at the white sky and I see the white is coming from me: I am breathing out smoke and I cannot help it, I cannot swallow it back. I know the Albanian is speaking the truth. His name can come from me like smoke and then my mother can die and I think I do not know how to go back to my country or what to say to my grandmother.*

*The Albanian boy is a leopard in a tree. He has his girlfriend under his loose hand; she is brushing her hair, white hair like dead grass in the sun. Hey,*

*Africa, say the Albanian boy, how you doing boy? He stretch out his paw, he takes my lunch tickets, he gives me my 50ps.*

*With that money and bus money I buy a sandwich no drink for lunch. I am kind to you boy, he say, kind, and when one boy go to speak to me, he say, leave Africa alone, he is mine. True, one time he give me extra money, say take the bus home. Kind. But all the time I feel his name behind my teeth, pressing like when they had the mashed potato for lunch and I could not understand it and the lady say gobble up. If I open my mouth to say one word, that name come out, like the potato, white with lumps, so I do not say one word.*

Every kid in the school, they know his name. They see him strolling, his trousers down here, his little wiggle, his little skank, then they call out his name. He's nice to them, yeah? Specially the little ones, the ones that can't cope. He takes care of them, yeah, puts his arm round them, gives them a hug. If they want cigarettes, he'll always go to the shop. He loves babies, honest, he don't never get angry except when they accuse him. Except when they say things he ain't never done.

Iz. Islam. Izzy. Yeah, it's an Albanian name. His dad give it him, yeah? His dad ain't over here. He ain't over there. I dunno, never met him. I don't know my dad either, it ain't a big deal. Why do you want to know?

*Soon I know that if a person speak to me, any person,
I will say that name. Tutortime, I sit with my
homework book. Breaktime, I walk the corridors,
busy, busy, tie neat, like I am going somewhere. In
class, if someone ask question, I nod, I write down
the answer. Group work, I go Notetaker role. Then
Miss Connolly gives me report: is Samuel talking? I
must carry it round, the teacher must say what I am
doing. So I stay at home. I spend the bus money on
bread. I cannot put heating on so I stay in bed, I
watch TV and I am there two weeks before they come
for me.*

Could've been anyone, dobbed him in. Depends who
they got hold of, ennit? The teachers, the Head. They
always go after him, try to put pressure on kids, put
words in their mouths. They want him excluded. They
want him arrested. Specially Miss Connolly, she's Head
of Year. She hates him, no kidding. She wanted him dead.
It's because he don't give in to them. Sticks up for himself. It's because he's special. Because he sticks out.

Like, they say, you been doing this and that? He just
goes, no, no I ain't, prove it. He says, this ain't Human
Rights, he gives it back to them, he says, be careful, I'll
get my lawyer on you, I'll get my friend. Anything happens, this school, they blame him. It gets to him, the way
they all hate him. Ain't nice, being accused of what you
ain't done.

*It is my tutor, it is Head, it is Miss Connolly, it is
another lady I do not know, she says she is Police.
They get my mum from her work, they have conference in the Head's Office. I am on a chair, my head
is bent, my mother is crying, begging me, they have
found mobile phones in my locker and they are stolen
ones and now I must say it is not me. I want to
speak, but I have lost the habit, I shake my head and
shake it, not me, not me, then my mother is begging
me, Samuel, speak! Her tears are free, they jump on
her cheeks like fish in a trap but mine are locked up.
My tongue is a snake, jabbing my teeth, it will say
the name and she will die. The Head is saying, talk
to us, and I go on my knees in the carpet, I raise up
my hands to the Head, and then the Head speaks the
name, he says, is it——? And I open my mouth and say
the name, and all the white spills out like milk, like
ice, and covers everything and freezes it, and nothing
can go on as it was before.*

It was the end of the day, all the kids standing out by
the bus stop, out by the road. It's a big road, four lanes.
He was having a fag, he was holding my hand. It was
winter, and the light suddenly turned on like a spotlight,
straight in our eyes, gold, low and hard. I turned, saw
the kids coming out of the school, the light on their
hundreds of heads, like waves, and Miss Connolly like
Moses, calling *Izzy, Islam.* Iz, I said. And he stubbed his

fag on the wall, and he kissed me, and said, see you later, then ran out in the road.

*There is a big noise, like metal, like the sky is a can and we have opened it. Then screaming. I am sitting on the floor of the Head's room. My mother is there. She is not dead. Everyone else has gone.*

He's a free runner. Do you know what that means? He can run up a wall. He can surf a road like a river. Runs between cars, over them, jumps off the boots. It's not dangerous, if you know what you're doing. It's because of Miss Connolly, by the kerb, shouting. That's why he lost it. And the light, maybe. The light in his eyes. He was looking behind him. It was a black four-by-four. They had music on.

*Then my mother comes and puts her arms round me, and outside the screaming stops. My mother has done this. That is what I think.*

He flew off the bonnet, and then it was a film. Trampolining, slow motion. The light – like picking him out. He bounced in the air with his arms up, fingers wide open, a dandelion clock, that's what I thought of, all the small seeds blowing. I thought: who turned off the sound?

*For a long time no one comes, and my mother sits*

*and tells me a story in my language, the old story of the river and his father the sea and how they wrestle in the rain, and how the river turns and runs away from its father, and how the sea hugs it and pulls it back.*

It was true love. Want to know how I know? The first time we did it, he picked up my hairslide, and put it in his lighter, and burned 'I' on my bum. Told you, I had a tattoo. It means I'm his, that's what he said. And I am his. Islam. I love him. I remember. It says so on my body. I know. Doesn't matter. You can't get him now. Can't arrest him. He's dead as a stone.

*So the river has brought me to the Unit, and here for tutor and teacher is Miss Brown. She has made special Maths for me, on the computer. I answer sum after sum, but in the Long Term she is looking for more Social Integration and I have written: I agree. None of this my fault: I have written, I agree.*

Sometimes I don't mind. It's quiet in here. Out there, in the school, there's always a fuss round me because I'm his girlfriend. Like I'm in a film all the time. Like I'm off the telly, because a telly thing happened for real.

*Now she has come to the Unit. Ashleen, his girl-friend. She does not know. She is very small, now, she is smaller than me and not beautiful any more.*

*She has cuts on her arms and her face has big red patches. She pulls her purple hair and rubs her pink eyes. Sometimes she is angry and old and sometimes she is young and says: I can't do it, I can't do my Maths, and then I look at her problem, and reach down the answer, a pot from a shelf.*

Sometimes I don't mind. I don't mind Miss Brown. I don't mind Africa, neither. He don't bother me, he does my Maths. It could've been him, I know that. Sometimes I think that. But he don't talk do he? Could have been Simon Harris, just as well. Sometimes I think, he could have written it down? But still, I don't ask him. I haven't, yet.

Sometimes I'm angry. Sometimes I do cutting. Sometimes I don't mind.

*Miss Brown is hopeful lady with ideas. Today her idea is a film of my country when I have finished Maths. The film is of a school in my country. Not a smart city school like I went to, a country school, they play in the earth, but there is the light, there are the boys in shorts, there is Maths on the board, there is the voice of my country, saying: Samuel Kuffor, this problem is for you.*

You finished now? You got what you wanted? Written it down, put it in your file. Made you feel better? No. It don't bother me. Don't matter to me, telling you that story. Why do you think it helps? The story's a story, do you know what I mean? You can tell it, but I have to live it. I wake up every morning and find it's still true. His body broken. His brains pale on the road.

*On the table I see Miss Brown's white dry hands and beside them my hands, black as the leaves on the road. I think: not all of these things can be real; me and Ashleen, my country and this country; the Albanian boy and my mother; the Unit and my school at home; the England voice and the voice of my country, the black hands and the white hands.*

*I am not real I say, and they are looking at me then, because I have spoken out loud, Miss Brown and Ashleen, pale eyes shining like money. You're real, Samuel, says Ashleen. For Chrissake, we all are.*

*For the first time she gives me my name.*

# The Show

Bit of a gypsy, then, Dale? said the Presenter of the Nation's favourite singing contest.

This was the auditions, and at first, people didn't realize what he'd said: there was barely a ripple in the huge dark hall. Dale wasn't fazed. He took the microphone and held it like a lollipop.

A traveller, he said. My Nana, she came from an Irish travelling family. And he moved the microphone away from his mouth, took a moment to listen to the echo of his speech, and smiled his soon-to-be-famous guileless smile. The crowd cracked and whooped like a huge tarpaulin bucking in the wind. Dale raised the mike and spoke to it again. But my Nana died last year.

His accent wasn't Irish, it was mildly Manchester: lilting, with broad, trustworthy vowels. He had huge brown eyes, thick-roofed and righteous as a calf's. Dale said: And this is a song my Nana taught me, and nodded sideways to the tech guys.

It was 'As She Moved Through the Fair', the Boyzone

version, but only the Presenter clocked that. Everyone else was imagining a tiny Dale in a caravan, being sung to by an Irish Grandma in a shawl. Oh, but it is a grand song, they thought, cod Irish accents inflecting their brains, and by the time Dale had hit the middle eight, they were raising their hands and lighting lighters, they were lost in a shared misty past somewhere on the Cliffs of Mourne. The camera panned steadily over their swaying shoulders, their upturned faces, their diamond tears.

Because of course he could sing, couldn't he, the bastard: it wasn't just the smile. Dale had a strong, boyish, husky voice that hit each note bang in the middle, clean as a bell; a choir boy's voice, as would emerge, trained, but not over-trained; a voice not so much broken as excitingly smirched: a voice that sounded, whatever it was singing, like the long-forgotten truth.

The Presenter, who had not got to be Presenter without a big dose of the smarts, recognized this. By the time Dale got to swan-in-the-bloody-evening, he knew he was utterly buggered. He was going to have to watch the whole thing over and over and explain it to the Board: him saying the fucking stupid gypsy thing; Dale slaying him with the song; the crowd stampeding their applause; and finally the judges, righteous and snide and putting the boot in. After he was replaced, the Presenter would sometimes play that last close-up on YouTube, late at night, in super slo-mo: Dale dipping his head and closing his long lashes like a curtsey, then raising them to gaze back at the crowd with absolute tranquillity and faith, as if they were his parents, interrupting him at play. It was really not the sort of thing anyone could have seen coming, a sort of sentimental perfect storm.

Not that Dale himself had any problem with the Presenter. I don't think he said it in a racist way, said Dale, warmly, on breakfast television. I think he meant, you know, am I Roma, cos of my dark eyes and that. But the reason I'm dark is, my Grandad was from Nigeria. My Nana, she had blue eyes.

Irish eyes? said the interviewer.

That's right, said Dale. There was another heart-breaking pause during which the Nation revisited the Cliffs of Mourne.

You see, said Dale. He'd have had on his fact sheet, about my family. I said about travellers. It's not a secret. So what I think is, he just made a mistake. I'm not angry with him. Dale was wearing a white shirt when he said all this, and studio make-up. Photos of him adorned all the red-tops the next day, and several serious articles followed in the broadsheets: *Travellers: living in the last ghettos?* And: *Gypsy: traditional term or racist slur?* Etc. Dale was just seventeen years old at the time, and looked in his mascara, as the *Indie* pointed out, like nothing so much as a baby seal.

Now the Chief Judge picked Dale to be his special protégée, and chose 'Irish Eyes Are Smiling' for him to sing in the first show. But Nana's eyes had been a hard bright blue, really, not much lashed. Nana had been very short and pink and fat and she made herself look older than she was: button-through overalls and helmet hair. Everyone had been surprised, at the funeral, to see her dates: just sixty-three. The Doctor said: if she'd spoken up earlier, they could have done something.

After she was ill, she spoke up, all right, she told everyone, anyone who would listen, any old social worker or nurse about her past: how she'd been a traveller, come from a big travelling family, and her Da had thrown her out when she got pregnant with the black fella, and the child had been a grand disappointment, which was no doubt her fault as she had been too young to know what to do. Dale would let her talk: he knew this story. When he was little, Dale used to ask for more, for a photo, for more about his black Grandad, for his Mum's name, even. Instead, the story always rushed to its ending: Nana had found the Church, she'd been given her grandson to bring up and he was a blessing even if his mother had gone to the bad, and she had never seen any of them again, no not a postcard.

The second show, the theme was *Divas* and Dale sang 'Say a Little Prayer'. It was his Nana's favourite, he told the judges, and the next day the *Sunday Express* did a big close-up picture of Dale on the cover and had: 'A Prayer for All Lost Children' as the headline. And so a Charity said, could they release a recording of Dale singing that song, to make money for little children with leukaemia and that, and Dale said yes, OK, he didn't mind. And of course they put Dale's picture on the CD cover and after that, the papers started hunting for Dale's secret life, because then it was Public Interest.

First, they found Father Gavin, Dale's foster-parent, but that was no good. Father Gavin was exactly the large, awkward, chronically inhibited man he appeared to be, and truly not much interested in anything but choir music. He didn't come to the Show on a Saturday because he had Mass the next day, but he did watch it on the television, yes, certainly. Further checks showed: Dale had sung in Father Gavin's tiny choir since he was six and played the organ every Mass since he was twelve; Father Gavin hadn't fostered before; Father Gavin had agreed to take Dale when his Nana died because she had asked him; Father Gavin was no sort of perv.

And that was it. Dale's mother was untraceable, his father unknown, his school attendance less than 20% and there were only so many photos you could take of Nana's grave. No girlfriends, football team, favourite teachers, mates, Yearbook, Facebook, Instagram, MSN. Nothing. Well, the last year you could perhaps understand. When his Nana was sick Dale had been, as one paper put it, an Unsung Young Carer, but the rest: where had Dale been? Father Gavin said: It was a hard sort of school, and I think Dale had issues there. But all the papers could find was an idiot on a forum claiming to be

Dale's high-school boyfriend, with an IP which could be traced to a Borstal.

Dale sang 'I Don't Like Mondays' on *Rock Night*, hopping about in a leather jacket. He was great, actually, what a song, but then of course the papers said, he was a bad role model, and on a charity CD too, and so the Chief Judge told him: You have to say something now.

So Dale went outside the mansion where the furry mikes made him think of Sesame Street and he said: I think young people should go to school. I wish I'd gone more often, because I made a big problem for myself. But I was trying to take care of my Nana. It was sleeting, and Dale smiled, and went indoors.

*It's a nasty sort of day*, was what Nana would say, when it rained. *Let's stay home and have ourselves a treat.* Bananas and custard, *The Sound of Music* on the video. Dale would play his keyboard, and they'd make up their own harmonies. Trifle and *Oklahoma!* Sausages and *West Side Story*. Nana could sing. She could sing really well: Maria, Rizzo, Ado Annie. A nice box of Roses and *Guys and Dolls*. Dale worked his way through all the roles: moving up from Miss Adelaide to Tony, Curley and Nathan Detroit. 'Luck Be a Lady'. 'Somewhere There's a Place for Us'. 'Oh, What a Beautiful Mornin''. *Show Boat*. The gas fire in the living room on full pelt.

Father Gavin's house was cold and bony, the furniture plonked down anyhow on a coarse moss-coloured carpet.

The mansion had shag carpets and underfloor heating, but still Dale shivered. He was always looking for a fire.

In his room, Dale curled on the floor. *Be my bright star*, said Nana in his head. They'd watched the Show together, made their plan. When Dale was old enough, seventeen, he'd win and buy Nana a house. And now Dale was doing it, and he would live in the house himself. The papers hadn't discovered anything really. Simon Taylor was in Iraq. Gameboy Wilson was in Borstal. Gaybot. Bumbandit. When Nana found the pig's head on the doorstep with its cock in its mouth, she had put on her rubber gloves and picked it up and wrapped it in plastic and put it in the bin. That's that, she said, and it was. No one knew. The papers wouldn't print that sort of stuff.

No one had found any photos, either. Maybe there weren't any, or maybe no one could recognize him, bland and middle-aged-looking in his V-necked jumper, sitting at the organ on the periphery of their family shots. They didn't know that Dale used to be fat, ten years old and ten stone, fifteen and fifteen. You couldn't win a singing contest at seventeen and seventeen, everyone knew that.

As soon as Nana died, Dale had known what to do, as surely as if he had a silver thread to keep his fingers on through a maze. He brought his keyboard from Nana's, the karaoke machine, and the bathroom scales. He carried them into Father Gavin's hastily converted study, and laid them out on the floor. The house was full of food from the funeral: pork pies and hula hoops. Dale ate a plateful, and drank lots of Diet Coke, then went to the bathroom and put his fingers down his throat till it all came back. It was the first time he had done this, but he'd read about it, and anyway, he was a natural, a talent. After that, the plan to be seventeen years old, ten stone, and a singer would blossom as a flower does, mathematically, petal by spiralling petal. After that, he could rest.

WILL DALE SEE MUM? shrieked the papers, next, and Dale said no, no thanks. They'd dug her up in an estate outside Edinburgh. Her name was now Melody: a dark, frizz-haired woman, with a little of Dale in the profile. She sang in pubs and footage of her doing this was circulated. She was good. She said she had never meant to give up Dale, but that her mother had taken and hidden him. She was a good mother to three new children. One paper lined up on her side, another on Nana's.

Dale took advice from the Chief Judge. He wanted him to do a duet, but Dale wasn't sure. Dale should have told the show all this about his background before they started, didn't Dale know that? Anyway, they did a deal, and Dale went to meet Melody in a room loaned by the TV studio with the cameras on. At first he couldn't see anything in her, she was just a woman, they talked about the show, and what he was singing on the Saturday, then all of a sudden she moved her hand to her mouth and said, oh, did you now? and reminded him of something.

The feeling was of being a bit of paper, folded in half by a giant hand. The sobs squeezed out. The woman called Melody who was his mother sat by him and begged him to take a tissue, but he wouldn't and in the end he asked to be taken back to the mansion.

Always, when there was a lot of noise around him, or when people asked hard questions, Dale could make it go quiet in his head. How do you achieve 20 per cent school attendance? You turn on a roar of blankness like an air conditioner: you smile like an angel. Nana wrapped the pig's head in plastic and put it in the bin. There now, she said, we won't worry about that. Dale crawled into his en suite bathroom, locked the door and knelt down over the toilet and reached his fingers down his throat.

Nine and a half stone, the scales said, the black stroke of the pointer shaking on the figures. Dale was a wafer in the stiff white sheets of the bed. But he needed soft bread to be sick, and a lot of Diet Coke, and now the photographers followed him to the supermarket, so he could only buy fruit juice and *Heat* magazine. At three in the morning, he went down to the communal kitchen and ate loaves of bread which belonged to a boy band from Lincoln. After he vomited, he slept.

The next day, two websites published accounts of the bread theft. They blamed the Girl Crooner. They put up her picture with the title BULIMIC? but it was only her lipstick running. Dale said to her it was disgusting,

disgusting, they'd say anything, he was sorry, but the Girl Crooner only looked at him, and moved away.

Father Gavin came to visit. Dale took him up to his room, and Father Gavin said: They've found your father, son. Or someone who says he's your father. Dale didn't respond, because if he started to talk Father Gavin would stay longer and he wouldn't be able to eat anything. He had some stuff in a bag under the bed. So after a while Father Gavin said: Are you going to meet him? And Dale said, no, not for now. And Father Gavin said that was understandable. When he left, Father Gavin held out his big ugly hand, and looked at Dale with an expression that was asking something urgently, and so Dale told him the song he was singing on Saturday, because that was a secret, that was what everyone wanted to know.

The song was: 'The Fields of Athenry'. Actually, it was *Film Night*, but the Chief Judge said this would be OK, it was in the *Dead Poets Society*, he'd even got Dale the DVD. Father Gavin said, it was only a fake folk song, did Dale know, phony history, it wasn't written till the 70s and that film was supposed to be 50s funny to think of, but Dale just gazed back at him, eyes smooth and blank as fish.

There was another speciality of that week: the contestants got to meet a real Big Star, one of the previous century's greatest entertainers and film stars now making a comeback, and sing to him in his hotel suite, accompanied by a white, lacquered, grand piano. The Big Star was much littler than you think: he had a small shaven head and a soft, lilting voice with an accent that had started in Wales and landed in California. The way his face wrinkled over his clever bones, his bright green eyes and extraordinary teeth with a diamond in them made Dale hold his breath: he didn't want to look any-where else. The Star was very interested in Dale, much more than in the others: he sat at the piano himself to play the chorus; he had him sing it again and again. Dale held the piano with his fingertips: the cool smooth solid-ity of it, frozen milk. He felt the notes come out of his whole body and vibrate like a flame, and the glorious feeling of that was mixed with a very great desire to touch the hot shaven pate of the Big Star, to hold that skull in his hands.

And so it was Show time, and in the audience now was Melody, but the papers had made her over and she looked like Shirley Bassey, and Dale's half-siblings and the small crumpled man who said he was Dale's father, and, ancient and enormous, hair growing out of his ears, Dale's great-grandfather, the man who had thrown Nana out. The TV Company made a package of all these people talking about having Dale back in their lives and they all wore T-shirts, *Vote Dale* and the phone number. Huge pictures of Dale singing and desiring and holding the piano started beaming around the immense studio, cheers and murmurs in their wake. Then it all went dark.

There was a single beam of white light on the stage,

and in it was Dale. He stood still, and sang: sang his song about a country and famine of which he knew nothing, a fake folk song which came from a film he hadn't watched. And as he sang the darkness filled with the bodies and outstretched hands of the dead, and the spotlight was the only pure thing, a ray of hope reaching across the world like the rainbow bridge to Valhalla. When the song was over, the audience screamed and applauded for a full five minutes, and the judges unsuccessfully tried over and over to reach over that sea of noise to get to Dale and tell him how profoundly they were moved and the camera flicked from them to the weeping Melody, to the crushed, motionless father, to the mountainous great-grandfather, punching the air over and over again.

Dale put on his cap and hoodie and made himself back into a boy. He moved through the shoulders and arms to get to the Big Star's dressing room. He had the same certain feeling, the same magic thread, as going to his bedroom with a bag of bread and Diet Coke. In fact, it had replaced that feeling, and Dale hoped this phenomenon could last, because he was tired to death of the vomiting now.

There you are, said the Big Star, at the door. But you'll have to wait while I get rid of these people. That took a long time, and all through it Dale sat quietly, in the dressing room, in the limo, and finally in a strange sort of basket chair which swung from the ceiling in the Big Star's hotel suite.

At last, the Big Star came and sat cross-legged at his feet. He smiled at Dale and his cheeks cracked, then he whirled Dale's chair, round, round again, and caught it in his slim, clean hands with the thick silver rings.

How long have you known? he whispered, the eye-tooth diamond flashing.

Known what? Dale said.

That you're gay, said the Star.

Just now, said Dale, and that seemed to be the right answer, because the Star picked him up in his wiry arms, and laid him on the bed and stroked him and at last Dale could hold that head and smooth its velvet.

And Dale did think he was that word. Gay. He had never denied it, never gainsaid it, not even to Simon Taylor and Gameboy Wilson. He could tell the Big Star about the pig's head now, if he wanted to, and be pitied for it. But that wasn't why he had come to the dressing room, not the thing he wanted to say.

The bed was huge and covered with quilted silk with glittering beads in the stitching, like tiny moles on good worn skin. The Big Star was good at undressing, and at undressing Dale: smiling ruefully, making a shimmy of it. Dale fell in love with his arm pits, their breath and tender hair. The Big Star was turning Dale over now, and he bit the pillow and let what was happening, happen. He thought, afterwards they could talk. About what it was to be a star, and shed yourself as light; spinning patterns from the blank at the centre of the self. About the golden scattering of a song; the sowing of its wheat on the endless dark fields of the crowd.

# Alas, the Tents Collapsed on the Green Field of the Mind

After she had her second baby, Laura relaxed the TV ban she had imposed on her first. She found she didn't mind, any more, if it stifled his vocabulary or deformed his brain, any more than she cared about washable nappies, or the news. No, every day, these everydays, when the little clock hand pointed to the twelve and the big hand to the six, she would settle little Christopher on his cushion, comfy in his well-peed-in, squashy disposable, put a sippy cup of pink juice in one paw, and switch on CBeebies. A twenty-minute programme was exactly long enough for her to feed the baby and for the child to defecate. Because there was another thing she didn't care about any more: Christopher could toilet train himself, if he liked, when he got to college.

Was Laura depressed? She had filled in a form about that and got a six. Perfectly normal, said the health visitor, for these difficult first months, and Laura passed this on to her old friend Marina, kind enough to phone.

The baby was called Andreas, but Martin called him And. *And-And.* When Marina made the same joke, *And, the second edition,* Laura ended the phone call.

Laura was, of course, breastfeeding. She intended to continue for three months, as she had done with Christopher. It was the best thing for the children. It certainly was not, she said to Marina, erotic. She didn't buy any of that stuff, not at all, any more than she bought La Leche, or a dairy-free diet. Laura prided herself on her scant and discriminating shopping. *Did not buy* was one of her phrases, just as *petite* was her size and favourite self-descriptor.

The children on the telly programme were in some sort of day-care, Laura noted. Very modern. She would send Chris, too, if she could find an establishment like that, furnished in flexible rubber and entirely staffed by children's entertainers always ready with the latest picture-book publication. The children weren't played by real four-year-olds, of course, but by adults in colourful suits and masks, padded to make their proportions right. The set was scaled-up to increase the illusion, but the coarse grain of their towelling skin was a dead give-away, at least as far as Laura was concerned. It bothered her: waxy, poreless cheeks were one of the things she did like, so far, about babies.

But the *PlayCare!* children were multi-racial – or blue, purple and yellow, at least – which was probably good for Chris now they had moved to what Marina called *the white suburbs.* And Laura liked the songs: jazzed-up versions of nursery standards. Once or twice she had even tried to get Chris to join in. The characters danced as they sang: the girl in pink specialized in high kicks of her great padded boots, and the boy-figure on the left, in the purple mask, stuck out his knees out and shimmied, just like Timothy Coombes.

The one on the left in the purple mask *was* Timothy Coombes. Laura was suddenly sure of it. There was Timothy's warm hoarse laugh, roaring out in response to the book about dinosaurs, there were his square, flexible shoulders, swivelling as he played hopscotch, there were his open gestures and cosy, close-to-the-chest air-punches, and the broad London accent he had used for the Pinter play, though really, he was quite posh, he had been to Marlborough.

So, when the baby was asleep, Laura googled: Who plays Dav-ee in *PlayCare!*? But there was no answer. The BBC didn't list actors: just the designers and producers of the *PlayCare!* concept. Laura tried Mumsnet, under *Children's Presenters*, but became disgusted by a discussion of who had the best bum, Giles off *Cook-a-doodle!*, or Tommy off *Pink Greenhouse*. She pressed Clear History, and went to change Chris's nappy.

Laura didn't even know Timothy Coombes, really. He was in his final year at college when she was in her first, but he had encouraged her to join the Backstage Gang at Freshers' Fair, and several times after that he had said

Hello, Laura, as she passed, raising his famous furry eye-brows in a dangerous manner, exposing his large even teeth. He was a little, bony person, like Laura herself, but this did not in any way impede his campus status as a theatre star and general all round stud. He'd look good on film! said Marina, then Laura's new best friend, giggling in a manner that implied that sex-tapes were nothing to her though actually she was a priggish shel-tered girl studying, like Laura, Law.

That summer, Timothy Coombes had taken his Hamlet to Edinburgh. The production was advanced, and had a symbolic set (Laura helped build the outsize encyclo-paedia he stood on to do 'To be or not to be'), and it got four stars in the *Scotsman*. They were all sure, then, that Timothy would be spotted, would soon be playing the West End. But 'Timothy Coombes' had no hits on Google since an appearance in *Doctor Who* more than a decade previously. His name on Facebook yielded a doctor in California and an orchid-growing grandfather in Kent. Laura thought perhaps he had changed his name: she'd heard actors often had to do that.

Or maybe this is what had happened to Timothy Coombes: maybe he had put on a felt suit over his neat pale bones and turned into Dav-ee. Perhaps the girl in pink had once played Viola, and the two parts of the spotty dog had studied with Jacques Le Coq. None of them had thought of this, then: of dancing on a rubber floor dressed as a monstrous four-year-old, performing kicks as high as a can-can girl's. But then Laura, who liked so much to be unencumbered, to travel with just one, perfectly packed bag, had never thought she'd be stuck on a sofa, wrapped in a baby, with a toddler slumped like a dog on her feet. The rubber floor yielded to the thick felt boots. And-And sucked vigorously and silkily, Christopher put a sticky, petal-soft hand up the inside of her trouser leg, and stroked, and Laura watched Dav-ee wiggling in the red shiny house. And then Laura felt something, the thing La Leche had threatened her with: a muscular arising inside where everything was so slumped and muddled since the birth; something like a slim, hollow stem growing, and parting, something which wanted to bloom.

When Timothy Coombes took *Hamlet* to Edinburgh, Laura hadn't ASM'd, because she'd already promised to go to Rome with Marina. But she did the prep. In those days, the players slept in the theatre, which was a Masonic Lodge, ordinarily, so Laura wrote everyone a note saying what to bring: sleeping bag, pillow, camping mattress (not lilo), and double-bed sheet. The sheet was to hang over the bed, draped on a rope suspended wall to wall, and tucked into the sides of the mattress to make a little tent. It wasn't practical: just for privacy. Laura had always liked that idea, the great room filled with little white triangles, and all that summer in Italy, in the economical Hostels for the Saving of Catholic Womanhood she'd cleverly booked through the guidebook, she thought of being under such a cover with Timothy Coombes. At night now, back to back with the increasingly meaty Martin – exhaustion made him eat, he said – Laura remembered the tents. In the murmurous room, in the wafting white, she whispered to Timothy, whom she now, like his inner circle, called Tims. It turned out he had always preferred the quiet type, such as Laura. He smiled with his eyebrows. He loved the parting of her soft brown hair, the many kind clever things her little hands could do.

Then the *PlayCare!* Roadshow came to town. In order to attend, Laura had to get her husband to take a day off work, and the baby to accept a bottle. Both tasks were difficult: Martin protested that it would make a great deal more sense if *he* went to the show, and Laura did the baby, and And-And, squealing and turning his head from the plastic nipple, clearly felt the same, but Laura tightened her jaw in the way that Martin knew, and Christopher knew, and And-And would learn, meant business. I need special Mummy time with Christopher, she said, and showed Martin the appropriate page in Miriam Stoppard.

So now Christopher and Mummy were having some: in the queue for the theatre loos, which was twenty mummies long. Chris had shat himself, and the tannoy was saying that the show would recommence in three minutes. Laura in her young days would have stood and fumed, perhaps written a letter, later, but her rage since the children was a wild west wind. That was something to tell Marina, one day, when she phoned with her melancholy enquiries as to what motherhood could possibly be like.

Watch this! Whoosh, Laura's rage opened the door of the Gents. Whomp! It threw Chris to the floor and whipped off his nappy. Crackle! It shook out a peach-scented nappy sac –

Hello, said Timothy Coombes, popping out of the cubicle. And Laura said Oh God, a lot, and sorry.

Timothy laughed. He was wearing an all-over grey Lycra suit, and his face was blotched red. He had also lost most of his hair, but he was very skinny, still, and there were his big teeth, his eyebrows –

Aren't you . . . ? said Laura.

Dav-ee, said Timothy. Yes.

No, said Laura. Hamlet.

Oh, said Timothy. And he blinked and looked quite different. I know you, don't I?

I'm Laura. From uni. You won't remember me.

Why wouldn't I? said Timothy Coombes, and then the call for the next act went through the theatre and he gave Laura his card. He had changed his name, just as she'd thought.

You look terrific, said Timothy Coombes.

\*

In order to go on a date with Timothy, now Lewis Kane, though she wasn't sure if he went by that name every day, and had scrupulously called him nothing on the phone, Laura had to take the children to stay overnight with her mother-in-law in Upminster. Fortunately, Laura had a talent for the furtive: Marina had once unkindly compared her to a cat on a litter-tray. All the time she was making her plans, she thought of nothing except the next thing. She had a fine thin little hum in her ears, like a fridge.

Everything went well: the lying about Marina's birthday, the packing, the bottle for And-And, the Noddy tape for Christopher, the sending for, and receiving of by express, a new dress from Boden. Laura took two calls from Marina during this time, both about Marina's current precarious relationship, and instructed her, during the second, to back her up in the birthday lie. Then it was just like old times: Marina wailing to be informed, Laura stubbornly refusing to say, both of them giggling and enjoying themselves tremendously. Laura's new dress had tight hooks at the waist: it was just the thing. Her mother-in-law waved her off with a bottle in her hand, and all the hour into town, jog-jog on the tube, Laura was alive, elegant and upright under her coat.

'Our hunting ground', Marina called The Cork & Bottle, off Leicester Square, though they hadn't done much hunting really. Once, they had chatted to some trainee doctors there, and, another time, a city chap had taken Laura's number. Now, Laura sniffed the air. She nosed her way there from the tube. And there he was, perched on a bar stool in his little jeans. Timothy, or perhaps Lewis.

Laura, he said, and did the eyebrow thing. I'm so glad, and he bared his teeth. And he bought her a big glass of wine, and for a moment Laura thought there might be a problem with what to say, the way there was on a Friday night, when Laura put the kids to bed early, and Martin brought home a take-away. But: Let's talk about *Hamlet*, said Timothy Coombes. And: The past is so erotic, isn't it?

So then Laura drank her Chardonnay very fast, and Timothy reminisced about the show, the whole crew, the sheer crazy ambition of those days, the work, the work, the amount they cared then, the amount they shared. He kept asking if she'd heard from Melissa, or Sheridan, but Laura didn't recognize many of the names. The wine burned the bottom of her stomach. Of course, she said, I was just the ASM. And I was younger than you.

It mattered so much, then, didn't it? said Timothy/ Lewis. Age. So silly. I still noticed you, though, Laura, didn't I? He moved his hand along the bar, till the tips of his fingers met hers.

Laura remembered sitting on the steps of the library, in shorts, when Timothy Coombes strolled by. She flushed to the roots of her hair. She let her fingers stay.

Oh, I so wish I could have gone to Edinburgh, too, she said.

Edinburgh? said Timothy Coombes. Oh, I didn't get there either. Not with *Hamlet*. I took a mime show, year after, but not the Dane. That was just big talk, little Laura.

But Laura had done the prep. She had seen the reviews. She had pinned them, with large black-and-white photos of Timothy in his kit, to the noticeboard in the English corridor. With the feeling of going down in a lift, and arriving at the same floor, of being locked in one of the surreal yet mundane dreams And-And woke her from, most nights, Laura realized this was not Timothy Coombes at all, and whipped her hand away.

Are you OK? said Lewis Kane.

I can't do this, squeaked Laura. And she hopped off her stool and ran to the loo, which was painted black and faintly smelly. She locked herself in the cubicle and wondered how she could ever have been so stupid. Timothy by the library had brown eyes; Lewis's were green-blue, and stuck out like he had a thyroid problem. She took out her phone, tried to frame a message to Marina, one that would make her predicament seem amusing, but got stuck on I'm in the WC at the C & B. She didn't press 'send'. She hoped Lewis would wander off after a bit, if she stayed long enough, but already she could hear someone outside the door, coughing. Laura flushed, and went out to wash her hands.

She was so tired. Even now, when you think she'd be mortified, actively ashamed, what had mostly flowed into the hole where her excitement had been was the treacly tide of her exhaustion. Once, when Laura was ASM-ing, she had been in charge of a set of life-size puppets. An art-student had made them out of stiff luminous paper, and each one was controlled by sticks at the neck and wrist by a blacked-out actor. It was a good effect, but the paper wasn't rigid enough, and every night one or other puppet flopped forwards, out of its joints. Since the baby, that was how Laura was too: always letting go of her sticks. In the mirror, now, she could almost see the thick silent shadow behind her, poking through in the black under her eyes and inside her wrinkles.

Of course, Lewis hadn't gone: he'd been drinking whisky and getting cross. He was leaning against the bar, cupping his face in one hand and tapping the fingers of the other in a way that let you know he was an actor, and Laura thought again how sad it was he had lost his hair . . . But Lewis tossed his head.

How's marriage then, Laura? drawled Lewis. Do you love him? Does he do it for you? I mean, like really do it?

All at once, Laura couldn't be bothered: Do you like Dav-ee? she said.

Lewis straightened up. Touché! he said and raised his glass. He looked at Laura. Come on, he said, and smiled. Sit down. And Laura hopped back on the stool.

I do like Dav-ee, said Lewis. Actually.

I like Martin, said Laura, trying to picture him and getting his teeth, brownish, clenched in a smile.

Lewis wasn't listening. You guys, he said. You *civilians* – that's what actors call you – you forget what it's like. You know? Making things. Art. Creating. Each time I go out there, in the studio, I'm creating Dav-ee. From scratch.

They don't give you a credit, said Laura. On the site.

He's still me, said Lewis. Making the show is totally collaborative. Very demanding. I studied with Le Coq.

Wow, said Laura.

*PlayCare!* is totally Le Coq! Greek tragedies were all masked! Any actor, any show, they're in a mask, only the mask is their face, said Lewis. And he smoothed back his ratty hair.

His nose was red. It had been nice of him to ask her out, thought Laura. It was nice that he fancied her. It flicked in her mind that she should set him up with Marina, and also that this was impossible. She said: The Roadshow must be fun?

Lewis shook his head like a dog shaking off water. So demanding! Totally, totally physical, you know. And mentally, carrying Dav-ee? He's a real person to all these little kids. It's beautiful? But hard. And little kids – they're where it's at, you know? They're so pure? Lewis was nodding to himself, like Christopher with his sippy cup. Well, he said, you know that, you've got them.

You don't? asked Laura, in case he was divorced.

I've got none, said Lewis. And I've got thousands. I've got all the kids who love Dav-ee. They're my kids. I love it. I mean, don't you love it, being a mum?

Sometimes, said Laura, I find it hard to love them right then and there. Sometimes, I can only love them afterwards, when I'm looking at pictures of them on the phone.

Lewis looked at her thickly, frowning, bothered. Jeese, he said. What happened to the little girl I knew at uni, eh? Laura wondered too: perhaps there was another tidy girl called Laura somewhere, pining for a tent with a hairy Lewis.

I've no idea, said Laura. Lewis groped for her hand. Laura let him.

They love Dav-ee, though? said Lewis. The kids do? Right?

Oh yes, said Laura, of course. Our *PlayCare!* times – they're the best we have, really. And she found it was true. The happy fact sat happily between them, a moment, and their hands stayed clasped, and then it was time to go. They were not sure how to part, so in the end they had a little snog, rather scratchy and toothy, in Leicester Square, and each got on their trains.

Laura had a text from Marina: How was secret date?? She texted back: Random!! Then she deleted Marina's texts, and Lewis's phone number, from her mobile.

She sat back. She hadn't brought a book. She thought

about Martin a while, but it was hard. She kept seeing his broad back in its white office shirt and her mind slid down and off it like a ski slope. At the bottom of the slope were the children, and she could love them at will, that was easy. She just had to picture And-And's three-quarter profile, Chris's upheld fat hand, and the feeling spurted up like an oil strike. She wondered how long it went on, this anchoring, energizing love, and what she would do when it failed.

After Barking, the train slowed down. It sighed at each station as if the engine had been replaced by a carthorse. She shut her eyes, and pictured the line home, not straight as it was in the diagram, but bending the way it had to, like water, nosing its way past things that were there and which used to be there, meandering round the backs of allotments in Dagenham, the outlines of the former car plant, the disused coal dumps and gas stations, and then through the buried rivers and lost field systems and defunct parish boundaries of the tiny Essex villages, all the way to Upminster, which had long lost its Minster, which was where she was staying, which was where she had now ended Up.

# The Girls

The main present is a playhouse: a huge, plastic, crenu-lated turret, complete with Gothic windows and pointy, purple door. Pink, says George, staggering away from it, and it is. Bubblegum pink. Sari-in-a-breeze pink. It glows against this rare blue sky like a chemical flare.

I settle small George in the sandpit with his small friend Sam. I settle myself on the swing set, and then up looms Alex, mother of Sam. They're all in there, she says, glumly, pointing to the pinkness. I nod, rub my toe in the dust, set myself swaying.

'All' means Alex's Ruby and my Ruby, our daughters (symmetry: we have to be friends), and Sarah-Louise. Sarah-Louise is related to neither of us, but her blonde and callow mother leaves her constantly in our care. This afternoon, I see looking around, she has done so again.

I decide not to mind.

I love that Saira has a swing-set, I say, leaning back. Hardly anyone has a swing-set, in England.

Alex stands with her arms folded. She is a tall, lumpy

woman, and she doesn't suit the heat – she has that thin English skin that blotches. She does not seem to approve of the swing-set, either, or perhaps it is just me, swinging. She is deeply suspicious of my upbringing in North Carolina. She thinks I spent most of it on a veranda, conspiring against Atticus Finch.

That's because it's usually raining, in England, she says, contemptuously.

Not today. Today is a blue day, a high, curved day, a party day. And here is Seema, the birthday girl, riding out from behind her new pink castle in her also new, also pink, corvette. She nods to us, backs up, pedals on. It's hard work. Her thin beige arms are tense on the steering wheel. She is dressed as Snow White – little yellow skirt, bright puff sleeves.

This dress, says Alex, plucking at her own skirt, is ridiculous. Ruby made me wear it. She makes a droll face, not a very good one, her small freckled skull jerking painfully askew on the fat flushed shoulders that never seem to match it. It is true that the dress does not suit her. It's ruffled, and made for a smaller, curvier, woman – me, for instance.

That's a tight fit too, I say, pointing at the playhouse. We can see the shadows of our children inside, pressed together in its rosy walls.

It looks toxic, says Alex. That pink. I'm sure it's not real. The house. I'm sure it's a Bombay knock-off.

Mumbai, I say.

Saira is from Lahore, anyway. And the colour is clearly integral. But Alex doesn't listen because a dismal squall now issues from the playhouse, followed by a sequence of bat-like cries. I would leave it to rise, for Ruby is my third child and many noises no longer bother me, but Alex stomps over, and peers into the playhouse, and pulls out Sarah-Louise, kicking her pink skirts and squealing like a Catherine wheel on the Fourth of July.

Sarah-Louise has huge blue eyes, and is kind of fleshy. Lush. Like a Victorian scrap, blowing soap bubbles or peeking over a cloud, decked with wings. She is prettiest, says Ruby, and I say, no, Seema is the prettiest of all the girls, she has eyelashes like Audrey Hepburn, and she is also smart, and she is also your friend, the only one you ever actually play with for more than ten minutes, but Ruby says, no, Sarah-Louise is my friend, her hair is gold.

Well, the gold hair is up round her head like a dandelion now, and her satin dress is smeared to the pink wall. Alex catches her up, too hard, too fast, and starts doing something with her skirts.

Is it a bee? says Saira, anxiously arriving with a tray.

No, I say, it's static electricity. And we giggle. Saira always giggles. I think she's only twenty-five.

Then the doorbell goes and Saira's family arrives in a river of women: mother-in-law, married sisters, sisters-in-law, unmarried sisters, all flowing down to the garden in their shalwar kameez, gauzy and appropriate in the sun, and behind them, a dozen cousins. Seema clambers from her car and joins hands with the little ones, and they run into the house like a chain of paper dolls. Sarah-Louise stops wailing, shakes Alex off, and looks after them, her brown belly sticking out of her pink satin skirt. She is surprised, I think, to have Seema run away so.

Alex is scowling too. But Alex has never been comfortable at Saira's, not as I am. Saira's house is one enormous back kitchen on a family bake-out – all those aunties and grannies shaking off their scarves and feeding the baby and asking when will your mother arrive to take care of your children properly. Always, I am charmed and Alex is not charmed: not even by Saira, with her daffy bob and unexpected, lengthy opinions on the issues of the day; her waving of a vague spoon by the stove and her grand letting of tea be served to all and sundry by the sari team; not even by Saira's baby, which is a long-lashed, frilly, film-star article, passed to you as dishes are passed, as spoons of spice, to savour and comment on.

But: I don't want to hold it, Alex has to say, stiff as a board. And why, because that makes the ladies sad, makes them ruffled and sorrowful as they hunt hurriedly for something else to praise.

Look, they say now, the cake! For here it is, being unboxed and laid out in the dining room, and we are processing towards it.

Nafeesa made it, says Saira. How clever.

The cake takes the form of a crinoline skirt, pink frill on pink frill of stiff icing, ornamented with flowers and silver balls. A Barbie doll – not Barbie herself but her brunette friend – with a tiara, is plugged into its centre. Her tiptoe, teeny feet and stiff legs and blunt crotch are thus, presumably, suspended in jam and sponge.

Christ, says Alex to me.

Oh, I say, but remember how hard it is to get your Barbie to stand up? Their feet are the wrong size! Wearing a cake could be a fine solution.

I say it to provoke, and it does: I am actually briefly concerned that Alex might spit in my eye. But now the children are sitting down, the boys on a football-themed table, the girls on a pink, bejewelled one. There is a special throne for the birthday girl, red velvet and gold, and, oops, who should be sitting in it but Alex's Ruby. Alex's Ruby has red hair and leaf-green eyes and is prettier than my Ruby. She would be very pretty indeed, in fact, without the powder-blue Cinderella costume and that small, down-turned mouth.

Alex says: Ruby, you have to go back and sit in your seat. Your seat, not Seema's special birthday seat.

I have to sit next to Sarah-Louise! wails Ruby. Sure enough, in the next chair, Sarah-Louise's impervious doll head, and, on the other side, my Ruby, in her pink puff sleeves, utterly thrilled. Alex wades over, kneels by the festal table like a plain and supplicant giant.

If you don't do what I say, now, says Alex, and we all hear her, I will smash up your Barbie doll. I'll stamp on her head. I'll put the bits in the bin.

Ruby shakes her head.

Alex grabs her pink collar across the table. Sarah-Louise, she hisses, is nobody. Do you hear me? Nothing.

And there is a pause. Ruby's little mouth is open like a slack marionette's. Sarah-Louise's long curled lashes sink to her cheeks, briefly, and rise again, and her stare is hard. Then Saira's mother-in-law, swans' wings of white hair on her black plait, says in her sweet sing-song voice: I think, after the singing, all the children may eat their cake in the garden. Shall we do that?

We do that. The playhouse really is a tight fit now. The walls bulge outwards, outlining the children, here a backside, there a head, the way a footpad presses through the uterine wall.

I bag the swing-set. Alex sits beside me, being kind of low on options, seat wise, after the crazed ogre incident.

I've given up my job, she says, I think by way of explanation.

Are you pregnant? I ask. She did something environmental, part-time, something underpaid.

No, says Alex. No. I am going to mother full-time.

Right, I say. For of course, there is no right answer to this announcement, nothing that will not give offence.

You see, she says, I have decided that if I want to bring

up Sam properly I have to . . . if I want Ruby to be . . . she waves her hand . . . to be a person. I have to . . .

I am watching George, who is rolling a huge, fronded plastic ball, like an enlarged pollen grain, slowly up the slide by the sand pit. He is three, now, interested in jobs. When the ball reaches the top of the slide, Sam, crouched at the bottom, calls out: Another load down here, please! And George lets the ball trundle down, then they repeat the process. They have been doing this for some time, perfect little mechanical operatives.

Alex has stopped talking. I say: Ruby seems real ebullient to me.

There are so many toxins, says Alex. In the environment. She is actually wringing her hands, as if to get water out of them. They are red and white as a checked dish towel. Especially, she goes on, in nursery. Capitalistic toxins, gender toxins.

Sarah-Louise? I say. Alex does have a case, there.

George has seen me watching. He trots over. Party bag? he says, hopefully. Go home?

No, says Alex, and she waves an arm widely and wildly. A harsh, bright, rash rises on her face, square across her cheekbones. She hisses: Don't you see it? Didn't you hope for better, when you were growing up? Didn't you think we were making a better world? Don't you care at all?

She isn't yelling, but she is a spectacle, all the same. Seema pedals over in her pink car and gazes at us, two cousins respectfully behind her. Screams from the pink house: the noise of brakes, of a balloon at full stretch. Just the three of them left inside there, now, I think: Ruby, Ruby and Sarah-Louise.

I mean, says Alex, gulping, turning her eyes away, straightening on the swing set. I mean, everything you want for your child, everything you worked and worked for, just burning up and being destroyed in front of your eyes? Don't you mind?

George turns to Alex, interested, informative. He says: Ruby said she would put me in a fire. She had fire sparks in her dress and she could burn us all right up. She said. So I ran away.

And he smiles at Alex kindly, and puts his cool, soft hand in mine, and I stroke it. I think how candidly, serenely beautiful he is, best-looking of all my handsome children, and that surely it will last, that wonderful ratio of forehead to eyes to mouth, and in time he'll be able to mystify many girls with his indifference, and make others cry until their features are entirely contorted.

We'll go now darling, I say. And I am about to ask Saira, coming down the steps with her scented baby, about the party bags, when Alex calls out, Look! Look!

The playhouse is moving. The children must have worked the moorings loose – you can see their feet, poking out of the hole in the base – and now they are holding the house up from the inside and running it round the garden, giggling as if the huge pink drum were filled with helium.

An accident, says Alex, there will be an accident! And she starts chasing the playhouse, arms outstretched, but it runs away, faster and faster, as if it really were magical, a Baba Yaga house, and soon the two of them are dancing, Alex and the pink tower, waltzing, as if the house were a crinoline, and the children were the bound feet, the red slippers, the enchanted shoes that will dance you to death. And of course it is only really seconds before the pink castle falls on its shining face, but those smoking moments on that shimmering day seem to last a long hour, and all I want to say right then to Alex, to all of it, is: oh, come on, come on, woman, doesn't that look like a good time?

# Shoes

I have a cold today, Joe said, first thing that morning. Mummy said, I have a cold.

Mel looked at him. Red eyes. Impacted snot over the upper lip. Much as usual, to be honest.

Daddy said, send him anyway, continued Joe. To get our money's worth.

Did he? said Mel.

Because Daddy has a special piece to finish. For the gallery. Are you going to call Mummy?

No, said Mel. Not now.

Mel decided to bear with it. She had been bearing with Jim and Hilary for some time now: with Jim and his 'pieces' and his endlessly defaulted upon 'Joe days'; with irruptions of grandmothers (both sides, both stupidly posh); with conjunctivitis and sties, and runaway, untended nits. From the start, Mel had borne with Hilary's frequent sudden work calls; and her opposite idiocies, such as arriving, barefoot in her office suit, in the middle of a picnic in Victoria Park.

Mel was used to biding her time. She pushed her small charges to the Drop-in, she pushed them home, and she fed them all beans. Mel didn't have many rules, but those she had, she stuck to. One of them was: she didn't take children with two full-time working parents. Actually, this was less of a rule than a manifesto. A USP. Everyone knew about it, in all of Stoke Newington, and even as far as De Beauvoir Town. But she always repeated it, when new parents came, and she had done so with Jim and Hilary. They had said they were both part-time, now. They had said they were both parents first, now.

In the afternoon, when Joe grew hot and feverish, she gave him two spoonfuls of Calpol and put him to bed in the emergency cot, resolving to wash the sheets on 90 afterwards. Another of Mel's rules: no colds. Because of the infection. She kept the other children in the garden, then let them watch the telly. She put all the Lego Joe had touched through the dishwasher, on *Hot: Pots and Pans*.

Do you enjoy your work? Mel had asked Hilary during her raid on the picnic.

Oh, said Hilary. Yes. I mean, I find it easy. You know, sums. I could always do sums. Easier than . . . this. She indicated the picnic, devastated on the rug.

This is the real work, said Mel.

Hilary nodded. Her hair stuck out wildly. Her legs were white as peeled sticks. Joe clasped her from behind, pulling her stiff skirt down over her bony hips.

Oh, I know, said Hilary. I know I should put on weight! The doctor says so. At this rate, I'll never have another! But I can't do it, I just can't.

And she wouldn't stop even for a bread-stick with hummus. She ran away across the grass, chasing a phone call, calling *I love you frantically, frantically!* to the wailing Joe.

But Hilary must love her work, really, or she wouldn't stay there so long. She was late this evening. All the mothers had come and gone. Mel didn't call her. She tidied up the Brio. She swept the kitchen floor. At a quarter to seven, Hilary turned up, and Mel let her stand on the step and apologize for a good two minutes before she even opened her mouth.

And then – well, it was surprising, Mel being such a sweet, even sort of person. The words flew out like rockets. Joe can't come back. *Psshw! Psshw!* Not tomorrow, not any time. *Bang! Bang!* Shells flaring on a dirt battlefield. Hilary's face blenched and shrank in the porch light as if it were punctured. Tears balled out of her eyes.

You don't like him! You don't like Joe! she said. And: But I have to earn the money, don't you see? Because no one else earns the money.

What had Mel said next? She couldn't remember. *There are more important things than money.* Yes. Because Mel believed that. She believed: *you can go back to the bank, but you can't go back on the young years with your children.* But had she said that, all of that, out loud?

She has no idea. All she can remember is Hilary shouting: *Do you think I want to do this?* and taking off her shoes, her black, patent, high-heeled shoes, and throwing them at Mel. Then she ducked her head, and Mel thought she was going to head-butt her. But she was only going to the back room.

When she came back, she had Joe over her shoulder, still asleep.

He's had two Calpol, said Mel, automatically.

It gives them asthma, said Hilary. She wiped her tears and nose across her suit sleeve.

He won't miss you, she said to Mel. Silly fat cow. She was crying terribly, and couldn't wipe her face because of Joe. It was raining, and Joe was only in his pyjamas, but Mel said nothing about it.

Mel stands, and surveys herself in the hall mirror. She smoothes her hips: her print skirt makes a perfect bell. The picture of a mother. That is what anyone would say. But Mel doesn't have any kids of her own.

Hilary's shoes are still on the floor, one by the sofa, one by the kitchen door. Mel picks them up, draws them together. Black patent, grosgrain edging, kid interior, quite new. Mel puts one hand in each, balls up her fists, and walks the shoes across the floor, one, two, three. But even her hands are fat, make stout, stupid-looking ankles.

Mel sits back on the floor. She looks at the front door.

She remembers Hilary stamping through it, out into the rain, Joe unwrapped on her shoulder. The child had opened his eyes, nuzzled close into his mother's neck, all his old-mannish anxiety gone, his face filled with utter bliss.

Well, there was a good thing. Mel stands up with the memory of it. She picks up the shoes, opens the front door, and puts them outside, neatly in the shelter of the porch, like empty bottles for the milkman.

# Animal, Vegetable

In this story, you have a particular friend. You've known her a long time – since college, at least, but probably even earlier. Maybe you both smoked Consulates out the window of the sixth-form common room. Maybe you went to primary school together, shared a desk, a pot of poster paint, an obsession with French plaits.

The point is, she's your high-achieving friend, the one whose exam results were always that bit better than yours, distinctions to your merits, A* to hard-won A. She's that bit more glamorous than you, too: a size down in jeans, hair naturally curly or naturally straight, whichever was in fashion the year you turned seventeen. No spots, no fillings. And this may have been hard to take, over the years, but no one could say she isn't loyal. When she got asked to the school dance, or prom, depending on your generation, and you didn't, by the boy you fancied, she insisted he took both of you, for instance, and that was kind, however badly it all turned out. And it was also nice that she wanted you to be her bridesmaid, even if weddings aren't your thing, and maroon is nobody's colour.

Anyway, by the time you are both thirty-five, partnered up and pregnant, she has this really good job. The job is very important to the question you will be asked at the end of the story, so please, apply your imagination to it strenuously. The job has an excellent salary and very long hours, but it should only be in banking if that's the sort of job you admire and are in yourself, the sort that you really approve of. Otherwise, make her the head of an important charity, fighting for civil rights, relieving famine, something like that. Or, if you're the arty sort, have her succeed in the area you most admire: make her a film-maker of rare and glorious distinction, or a theatre director, the nation's finest, something on that level. And give her husband the just-same sort of job, but ten years senior and even more demanding and well paid. He's her first boss: a very much top-drawer type, driven, bit distant, very trim and elegant. Your partner is your college boyfriend and he usually has egg on his trousers. He also has round shoulders, and enthusiasms so boundless you sometimes worry they are random. As for your job, I'm afraid you've just lost it. Yes. Redundant when pregnant – that old story, but cleverly done. Don't even think you could sue.

At least the redundancy means, though, that when your baby is three months old, there is no question of going back to work. Because, let's be honest, they wouldn't let you through the door. You're at least three stone overweight, and still walking funny and wetting yourself after the emergency Caesarean. Your breasts are cushion size, and leak, especially the left one. You have forgotten what it is to sleep at night, and despite all the breast milk, your baby has eczema so bad you are deprived of all compensatory baby prettiness and silkiness and general admiration – old ladies stooping to look in your pram jump back, repulsed. Your house is a mess, your confidence at an all-time low.

Your friend comes round. She says the Pilates really helped her through her water birth, and definitely with getting back in shape since. She shows you her baby, slender, muscular and bright-eyed as kitten, and the tiny creature meets your eyes and smiles. Andrea. Your friend is enlarging on her future plans. She has hired a nanny. She was dealing with work documents within a few hours of the birth, and now she is going back full-time. Andrea is ten weeks old.

What about the breastfeeding? you squeak, for you are preoccupied with feeds and how you could possibly get the baby to have his main one in the day, not the night. I moved over to bottles, she says, coolly. She's had her six weeks. You say nothing, but you eye up her neat blouse and find yourself chewing over this pronouncement, often, during the next few months, especially when you have the mastitis, and when you switch to the millet-only diet, the one you find does nothing for the eczema or your figure. At La Leche, you make a new friend, a solid, militant Finn called Ulli, and confide in her about your old pal with the nanny. It is horrible! says Ulli. The child will have no antibodies! She will not bond with her mother! She will grow up with a hole in her brain. Which is what you'd hoped she say.

But little Andrea has skin like a rose petal, and she is very well-bonded with her nice, intelligent, well-paid, permanent nanny, who you see in the park frequently, who takes Andrea to music class and baby gym already. The nanny keeps you up with the milestones: Andrea smiles, crawls, walks, runs, hops and speaks earlier than your child, and better. At Andrea's second birthday party – to which you are invited, for you are never forgotten – her mother says to you: You mustn't think I don't admire you for doing it all yourself: I really think that's a wonderful choice. But I just couldn't do the, you know, animal vegetable bit. The farming bit. For me I find that now Andrea is speaking, we can really form a relationship. I'm finding she's such a great person.

You're pregnant again, at this point, the shape of kohlrabi. You are still untidy and disorganized and poor and you are increasingly bad-tempered. The toddler is a fussy eater, and you are inclined to feed him baked beans and white bread, and then feel angry with yourself about it. It is impossible to say that Andrea is disadvantaged in any way by having her Nanny feed her on fresh vegetable soup, dried apricots, and pomegranate juice. She is starting the violin. It is impossible to say what is good about your choice, this mucky, short-term, animal life which seems to have been going on for ever, this round of viruses and exhaustion and E45 cream which the child will not even remember. You call Ulli, and she tells you that the first three years with a child are psychologically the most valuable, and throws in a sad story about neglected monkeys making bad mothers. You decide to solve the problem by not seeing your friend any more, or, at any rate, not till you've got your figure back, which is the same thing.

But you underestimate her, her kindness, perceptiveness, loyalty. When you have the second baby, she comes round with gifts, she arranges several days out with Andrea and the nanny for your peeling, be-spectacled, and now extremely jealous and angry toddler. She says she is quite sure that all children bite. She says she wishes she had another child, but that, genuinely, she does not have the time and the resources, and this sounds to you like a true and regretful and also admirably self-knowing statement. She holds your baby with real tenderness, and, when he is six weeks old, she sets you up with a little bit of freelance work you can do from home.

Which definitely helps. Whatever Ulli says. A bit of contact with the adult world, emails marked *important* (!) arriving for you. You even stagger into the office and make a small presentation, squeezed into a three-year-old jacket, and feel lifted by it. It's all easier, anyway, the second time around. The baby has a lovely nature. Or maybe it's just not having eczema. Or just that you're not so crap at the whole thing, any more. You start the toddler at nursery three days a week, take on another small job, don't see Ulli so much, and when you hear that Andrea is starting prep school, that she can play the flute, when you receive letters actually written in her four-year-old hand, you manage genuinely to be pleased. You say to Ulli: I really think that as feminists we need to respect each other's choices; and tune out when Ulli starts on about the class aspect of life in England, and how the longer she lives here, the less she can stand it.

In fact, by the time you hit your fortieth year, your friendship is so happy, and so calm, centred, and even a bit thinner are you, that when your old friend scores a huge triumph in her job, makes headline news, and starts to work in Paris, you are thrilled, and defend her to your partner who is having a weirdly conservative moment. Her work is a true inspiration. It shows how women can work better after childbirth, and besides, your friend is at home with Andrea every weekend. They have carefully defended quality time, and sometimes you are asked to join them. When your birthday rolls round, you have no problem with inviting the whole set, Mother, Father, Daughter, and Nanny, to your actually rather laborious get-together in a Youth Hostel in the Brecon Beacons.

They're frightfully nice about it. They drive all sorts of places, and the nanny looks after ten children so you can go to the pub. Andrea and her mother are great together, even though the kid has a cold or something – easier, honestly, than you and your still-itchy, still-mulish, still not specially bright older son. And, over the third pint in the Welsh pub you think: OK, let her have it. The job, the kids, the money; cheers, my friend. And you toast her, over your smeary glass.

You don't say anything of course, but your friend must sense your change of heart, because it is to you that she turns just a few weeks later, your messy kitchen in which she suddenly appears, incongruous in her silk shirt and suit.

This is the story. In the last few months, Andrea has been getting clumsy. The nanny noticed it, and the teachers. She's been dropping things – balls, toys – she's been finding it harder and harder to hold a pen, she has had problems getting dressed. When she walks, she stomps, on her heels. Recently, her speech, always so clear, has seemed slurred, especially when she's tired. In school, she puts her head on the desk, says she has forgotten words she has been able to read for years, sleeps. Both your friend and her partner have loads of health insurance, and so the nanny has taken the child on a round of medical appointments. And now they have a diagnosis and this is it:

Andrea has an incurable, degenerative, genetic disease of the nervous system: something like Huntington's but much more unusual. An ataxia. A rare variant. Your friend repeats the name of the disease and the number of its variant several times, but you can't take it in. You're thinking: *my child stomps*. And: *is it catching?* You need to stop that, and drag your mind back to Andrea. What is happening is: her brain cells are dying and not renewing themselves. This is the prognosis: rapid. Andrea will be in a wheelchair in three months, quadriplegic in a year, unable to swallow in eighteen months, and unable to breathe (dead) within two years.

Now you are thinking: *If Andrea has it, my kids can't get it. Stalking horse, scapegoat, sacrificial kid.* Then you think about Andrea: clever little Andrea cross-legged on the floor, reading a book, and you imagine the words swimming in front of her eyes, the wobble in the legs, the hands, and you want to throw up. You sit down at your kitchen table and take your friend's hands. She is still talking about the diagnosis. What happens is: the cerebral cortex dies first. Andrea will lose her speech and her higher intellectual functioning before she loses the rest of it. Probably in the next three months. So, by the time she is reduced to animal level, being spoon-fed in a cradle, she won't know it. That must be a mercy. When she's back in nappies, she won't know who is changing them. Animal, vegetable. Farming. A body. The nanny has said she will stay on.

You pour your friend a whisky, and one for yourself. It's three in the afternoon. Your hands are shaking. And here comes the question. It's about the job. Your friend has three months' compassionate leave, but after that, she needs to be back in Paris, because after that the project will die. (Remember, it is a *great* project. You admire it on every possible ethical and artistic level. And she is the only woman for the job.) Should she give up her work? She's really asking. For the first time in your long history, she doesn't seem to have worked out the answer in advance. So, what do you think?

Yes, that's the instinctive response, but *think* about it a bit more. Engage your brain, the way she always does, the way you don't. Why do you think that? Why her? Why now? Who benefits?

Now, open your mouth and tell her. Tell her why.

# The Not-Dead and The Saved

* They've been asked to wait in Paediatrics. It is five o'clock, already; and the sun is streaming in through the high, unopenable windows. Thrum, thrum, thrum, resounds the concert in the Day Room, and his name is Aitken Drum.

The Son is lying on top of the blanket. He has lately taken to wearing aggressively small jeans which he customizes with black thread and biro drawings in the style of Aubrey Beardsley. He taps his dirty fingers on his ripped T-shirt. His large, glittering brown eyes sweep the empty ward.

Look, he says, in his new, adolescent, scratchy voice. A Not-Dead.

What? says the Mother. The Mother has been putting off her tiredness for so long that it tends, like a neglected middle child, to leap at her at the least chance. Just now it is sitting on her lap, arms tight around her neck, breathing the scents of Paediatrics into her mouth: strawberry syrup, toasted cheese, pee.

A Not-Dead, says the Son. Look. Under the window.

Mother cranes round. She sees a baby sleeping in a plastic cot. It is wearing a pink woolly hat and cardigan and has oxygen tubes in its nose.

See? says the Son.

It's a baby, says the Mother, crossly. Someone's baby. But the baby's eyes are too far apart, and it has a cleft palate, and its whole body has a flattened, spatch-cocked look, as if it is trying to separate into two pieces, East and West, and the Mother is already worrying that there might be a crisis and she will be called upon to Do Something. The Mother is not a good choice for the parent of a chronic invalid. She is inhibited and impatient (often both at once) and she fears sick things: fallen fledglings, injured cats. Someone else always has to pick them up. Her ex-husband, preferably, who is bluff and easy with illness, who would carry the Son casually around the hospital in his arms, the tubes draped jokily but handily over his shoulders – talents he is now wasting on a new, completely well, wife and child.

She should be dead, says the Son. Like in nature. I mean, if that baby was born in a primitive tribe, she'd be dead in seconds.

So would lots of people, says the Mother. So would I.

I would, says the Son. He raises his fists to his forehead, surveys the puncture wounds inside his elbows, and adds: I'd be the deadest. The Mother sighs. Once, the Son was prodigious and original, and the Mother was

daffy and whacky, and they were on the same side: now
they seem doomed to partake in endless EFL Oral Exams,
with the Son taking the part of the difficult student, the
one with the nose stud.

You were a perfectly healthy baby, she snaps.

Not really, says the Son. Only *apparently*. I was born
with it, remember? My tumour. That's what the new guy
reckons.

Oncology is a new favourite subject. So is genetics,
and blame. The Mother decides not to meet the Son's eye.

Anyway, she says, we're not primitive.

No, says the Son, leaning back on his pillows, we've
got the technology now. And cos we have the technology, we have to save her. The baby. I mean, the Doctors
and people, when a baby like that is born, they have
to save her. It would be *wrong* to ask them not to save
her, I can totally see that, cos then they would be like
murderers.

And? says the Mother.

So then the person they save is not dead, but sometimes they're not alive either. Like they need the
technology to keep them going? Like they can't be properly alive, but no one knows what to do with them?
Not-Dead. See?

The Mother wakes up. She scents danger. She leans
forward, and the Son fixes her with his shining eyes.

I see them everywhere. You know? Not just in the
hospital. Some of them are in disguise, but I can spot

them. Like they have a little shiny outline round them, like in a game on a screen. They pixelate, Mum, they pixelate at me. Like: there, there, there. Shouldn't really be here. You, you, you. Not really here. Me, me, me. Not-Dead.

No, says the Mother, loudly, unsurely. You're alive.

I'm not dead, says the Son, because of the Machine. But where am I alive?

In your mind, says the Mother. You're alive in your mind, that's the thing. The life of the mind.

Because the Mother believes this most sincerely. And so, during the long while they have to wait for the plasma and the trolley, for the Machine and the nurses, the Mother babbles about Robert Louis Stevenson, also sickly, also bookish. Then she enumerates to the Son the titles of all the books he loves the most, all the books they've read together, their favourite episodes, and, after a while, the Son says, You know *White Fang*? I was thinking about that. I think it's, like, a prequel to *Call of the Wild*. White Fang is Buck's grandfather. You can work it out. There are, like, all these little clues.

Then he curls down on the pillows, and chatters on about the great dog Buck, and how he is actually fulfilling the White Fang's dream or maybe, like, the call of his *genes* when he runs into oblivion in the Canadian woods, and daringly the Mother takes his hand and folds it inside her own and remembers how soft it was when he was a little boy, really as soft as a petal, the curved veined petal of a magnolia in its brief springtime brilliance; and all the while the baby breathes in its tubing, its arms abandoned by its sides, its ribcage moving up and down with exaggerated depth in its pink covers, a giant, disconnected, heart.

* Three weeks later, they are in Acute General. They can't be in a single room, because of the price of nurses. Because nurses have to watch him, now. Because, yesterday, the Son unplugged his Machine and watched silently as his life blood was pumped to the floor. And where was his Mother? His Mother was on her way to the library, that's where, because her Son had said: Go and find a job, a life of your own, that's why. She was nearly there when she turned and sprinted back. She doesn't know why.

Now they have pumped pints of blood back into his veins, now they have re-inflated his internal organs and wheeled him out of the ICU. Now the Mother and Son are going to have their first conversation. The tubes are out of his throat, but they seem to be in hers. They are in a bay with the curtains drawn. Acute General. Anyone could overhear.

It was an impulse, Mum, he says to the ceiling tiles, his voice hoarser than ever. One of those things. Try not to fixate, OK?

How can it be an impulse? hisses the Mother, furiously. To bypass six security systems?

Oh, I worked out how to do that ages ago, carols the Son. Sort of like chess. You know?

The Mother taught the Son to play chess herself. Yes, she can see how he could do that: work it all out. And already, just two moves in, the Mother starts to weep, and the Son looks at her, then away.

The thing is, Mum, says the Son, picking his nails, you got it wrong.

The Mother is prepared to accept she has got many things wrong. Which one, though?

Robert Louis Stevenson? says the Son. Remember? He just wasn't that ill, Robert Louis Stevenson. He could walk. He got to have sex. He grew fucking up. Mum. Not – The boy gestures at his feet, sticking up in a little tent of blanket halfway down the bed.

The Mother slumps out of her chair and puts her head on the end of the bed. She is thinking about her love for her son. It was born at the same time as him, and she is not in control of it. She imagines it as very strong and not at all intelligent, something that moves about in the dark and grabs things. It has claws and tiny eyes, like a lobster.

But your transplant, says the Mother, it could be any time. Next month.

Yeah, says the Son, exactly. And they both remember the last transplant.

What about me? says the Mother, after a while, sitting back on her heels. What would I do without you? How would I feel?

The Son sighs deeply. Mum, he says, you have to see, don't you? You have to see that I can't be responsible for that?

* Paediatrics, again. They've been called in for the transplant. The Son beckons to the Mother conspiratorially.

Look, he whispers. It's the Not-Dead baby.

The Mother peers through the gap in the curtains. In the opposite bay, flanked by machinery, are a cot and a pink-clad shape.

Are you sure, says the Mother. It's the same one? That was months ago. Wouldn't she have grown?

Mum, says the Son. Haven't you learned anything? Of course she wouldn't grow.

Now a woman stands up, and draws the curtains of the bay. In the slice of light they glimpse the shadow of her belly.

I hope she didn't see us, says the Mother.

Did you see her? hisses the Son. Pregnant! Holey moley! and he collapses theatrically flat against his pillows. The Mother finishes pulling out her sofa bed, and lies on it. The Son is staring at the ceiling, and has not re-plugged the iPod.

Is it bad that she's pregnant? she says, after a while. In Paediatrics, there are pictures on the ceiling: Piglet and Pooh, walking into the sunset.

No, says the Son, but it's weird.

How weird?

Well, that baby is going to die. The Not-Dead one. I think it has Edwards' Syndrome. I looked it up. So that baby will die, and then, just at the same time, she'll have a new baby. And then what will they think?

Maybe, says the Mother, though it is a bothering thought, they'll think they've got a new baby to love?

Yeah, and maybe they'll think the old baby got a new body? You know? Transmutation of souls?

Would that be bad?

Not like, Hitler bad, but it is fucked up. Because, what I think is, your soul doesn't exist. Your mind doesn't, even. Your mind is a bit of your body. It's just the same. That's what the Prozac tells you, Mum. See. Look at us. We've taken the pills, and they've changed our bodies, and that's changed our minds. Here we are, having the transplant, happy campers. Different souls. See?

Yes, says the Mother, who has brought zopiclone with her and is about to take one. I do see that. I see that point.

I'm going to put the light out now, says the Son, and does. In the dark he says, in his Dalek voice from way back, from his *Doctor Who* phase: Tomorrow, I get my transplant. Then, I start to grow. I am on drugs that make me optimistic, so this is easy. Goodnight, mother-unit.

The Mother's pillow smells of rubber. The wall next to her head is padded vinyl. When the Son was little, she would lie here in Paediatrics and tell him they were camping out, in the Dormobile, lost in the French countryside. She tries to tell herself one of these stories now, but can only think of the Son's illness, the long road, the many forks, and how, at each one, they have borne inexplicably left, further and further down B routes, nearer and nearer the sea. Recently, several people have told her that the Son owes her his life, but the Mother doesn't feel that at all. It is she who owes him his, in the same way you owe a child a good picnic, when it is your idea to set out, and you who forgot the map, and now you are lost and there is no hope ever of the rain turning off.

* This is a new hospital, in the city where the Son now goes to University. The Mother had to get a taxi and a plane and another taxi; she had to ask at two reception desks; a junior Doctor met her at the second and is now trotting beside her; he is saying the crisis has peaked, and new antibiotics and best foot forward, hopefully; but she can hardly hear him for the fire-doors swing-swinging in her head; and here they are: Cardio-Respiratory.

The Son is already stable. He is sitting up in bed, attached to, for him, a minor amount of apparatus. He will always be small, but his cheekbones are good, he is bonily handsome. Lollipop head, he says, of himself,

I should be on TV. There are girls, now, and here is one beside him, importantly holding his hand. She has blonde hair in plaits and liquid dark eyes and an animated, deer-like way of holding her head and back. The Mother makes the mistake of automatically discounting her and sinks onto the bed, her mouth open, her hands stretched out, her body pulsing forward, ga-ga-ga-ga, my dearest love.

You don't need to worry! cries the Girl. He's come through! They never saw such a spike in the graph!

And the Son gives the Mother a quick lift of the eyebrow and an embarrassed smile. He raises his hand but it is encumbered with tubes and with the girl's hand. He is about to drop out of college and marry the Girl; he is going to live on an organic farm with a group of medical emergency survivors called The Saved; he is going to give up meat, alcohol, and irony and assume white robes and quasi-Zen belief; he is going to surrender to the leadership of a tall, wintery, ex-kidney-patient named Attila; he will tell his mother that he is dedicated to the celebration of the moment and meditation and macrobiotics and this is why she cannot visit him or speak on the phone; he will explain that all this is done with his free will and is legal and not a cult and that Attila has plenty of experience with private detectives; the resulting period of constant acute tension and mourning will last more than three years; and though his gesture may start as an embrace, it ends as a flat-handed, Popish, stop-sign.

* A third hospital. This ward is *Acute Assessment*. Here is the Mother who has just sat down, and here is the Wife on the opposite chair. The Son is propped up on pillows with his eyes shut. His hair has come out in tufts, now, and his skin is yellow-green and mottled like slip-ware. Now he is thin as a November guy.

The Son opens his eyes. Something has happened to them: they have curdled or solidified, gone from beer, full of yellow lights, to toffee. It must be the Wife's fault. The Son doesn't greet the Mother. He says to her: It's the baby. I can't stand the baby.

What baby? says the Mother.

His baby, says the Wife, pointing to a toddler playing in a shaft of sunlight on the other side of the ward. The light catches the filaments of his hair. A path of trembling air opens up between the Grandmother and that little dandelion head.

He wants juice, says the Son. Then he wants milk. Then he spills it on the floor. Then he howls. I mean, is that reasonable? Does it strike you as reasonable behaviour?

When did you have the Baby? asks the Mother/ Grandmother.

Don't you mean why? says the Son.

He's fourteen months, says the Wife. He was born at

the Farm. A water birth. She makes a calm blank face and looks straight at the Mother, as a cat turns towards its enemy the blind spot between its eyes.

I'm taking Jaybird back to the Farm now. OK? she says. But the Son has his eyes shut. Too late, the Mother runs after the Wife and at the Ward door she puts her hand briefly on the Baby's head and tries to smile but it comes out as a moan.

The Son opens his eyes for his Mother. They think I have a brain tumour, he says. They're really pretty sure. Maybe even more than one brain tumour, they're going to do a scan. Then they might want to do chemo but I can't be bothered, I mean, what's the point, do you think?

Is that why you're angry with the Baby? asks the Mother. She knows this doesn't come first, but the heat of the Baby's head is still burning in her palm. The trout, love, thrashes in her chest.

How should I know? says the Son. How can anyone know that, Mum? And then he vomits on the floor, and fits, and his Mother, still squeamish after all these years, doesn't know where to touch him and presses the alarm above the bed and the Doctors come, dozens of them, more than even she has ever seen.

* In Oncology, the Mother is shown images of the tumours. There are three: bore holes or storm systems or black beetles in the bright contour maps of her son's

brain; and the Consultant wants to operate or at the very least shrink them with chemo or radio. The Son is refusing all treatment, but, as the Consultant says, he is not himself and should perhaps be Sectioned.

No, says the Son, to the Consultant. This is really me. This is actually how angry I am. I am actually this angry with hospitals. I really do hate you. You are not doing anyone any good and I do not give you permission to put your fingers in my brain.

But it is true he is also angry with everyone else. He can't remember why he asked his Mother to come, and keeps shouting for her to be taken away. When Attila arrives, in his clean white nightie, carrying Tupperware boxes, the Son refuses to let him lay on hands, and calls the proffered macrobiotic curry a cow-pat. The Mother, watching from the next bay, smirks, and in a whirl of white, Attila catches her arm in his hairy hand.

I'm going to tell you a story, he says, as the Mother blinks into his large-boned, plain face. About laughing. My *roshi* had a tumour in his arm. He watched it grow, and he said to it, tumour, you will be the death of me. And then he laughed at the tumour. At first, we could not understand, but then we laughed with him, and after some days of laughing the tumour shrank and dis-appeared. I saw this with my own eyes. Now, laughing woman, will you laugh with me? The Mother is shaking her head but Attila opens his big bearded mouth and laughs, mirthlessly and loudly, showing his teeth, big as a donkey's.

Holey-moley, says the Son, and pulls his blanket over his head.

This, to the Mother, demonstrates that the Son is sane. But next, in comes the Wife, with the Baby (the Baby has a chemical effect on the Mother's vision whereby he is illuminated and everything else turns greeny-orange, like an old TV screen) and the Son turns his back on them and buries himself in his pillow. When the Baby tries to tug it off with his little plump hands, calling funny dada, the Mother witnesses the Son knock the Baby over on the lino, and in the stramash that follows, the screaming, fits and forcible injections, she coldly thinks that perhaps the Son should be Sectioned, after all.

Now the Mother sits by the Son's bed while he sleeps. When he wakes, his eyes are clear.

You were right, says the Son. We shouldn't have had him.

I didn't say that, she replies. How could I? I wasn't there.

You didn't need to be, he says. I internalized your response.

It is indecent, how much this pleases her.

But you love him, she says, hopefully. The baby?

I expect so, says the Son. But I'm letting him down. You see?

Yes, says the Mother. It's a terrible feeling. But the Mother is smiling, because she is still looking into her boy's eyes. Over the years, she has lived with many imaginary versions of the Son – a spry, unmarried one, most recently – but also a heavy-limbed footballing boy, also a big lad who picks up her bags at the station, easily, as if they were empty, also a grown man who lifts her off her feet, tight to his cashmere chest, and all of them have had these eyes, eyes with gold lights, with pinpoints of the true dear dark.

Because this time, says the Son, I am going to die. And you have to let me. You really do.

* In the Hospice, the tumours eat the Son's brain rapidly, like chalk cliffs eroding in a storm. Things fall off: houses, people. So, when the Wife comes in, the Son turns to her and smiles and her face opens in joy.

Hello, says the Son. Have you come to visit me?

I brought Jaybird, she says, indicating the child.

Is he yours? he says.

The Wife leaves the hospital at once, the Baby like luggage on her shoulder, and gets in a taxi, the Mother at her side all the way, pleading.

It isn't you he's forgotten, says the Wife. And the Mother feels a goldfish flick of pleasure.

The tumours eat words, but for a long time they are unable to devour music. So, round the Son, everyone sings: 'Food, Glorious Food', and 'Dance for Your Daddy'.

For, in a single night, the tumours have swallowed fifteen years of bad feeling against the Father. The Mother has called him, and he has come, salt-and-pepper-haired, now, prosperous and contented and wearing sports shirts the Mother would never, not in a million years, have allowed him. In he strode and picked up his Son in his arms and the Son, barely audibly, started to hum *my bonny laddie* . . . Everyone, even the case-hardened hospice workers, wept.

The tumours cannot eat chess, and for as long as the Son can lift the pieces, the Mother plays with him. It induces healthy synaptic activity, say the doctors, and she should keep it up. The doctors do not think the same of *White Fang*, but the Mother reads it aloud anyway. There are pathways in the brain, she thinks, for her sledge and its dog. Deep down in the brain stem is a pebble which is the Mother and the Son, and this is where they are headed. The pebble is ivory and has an embryo etched on it, curled. 'Speed Bonny Boat', sings the Mother to that embryo, and 'You Are My Sunshine'. All those sad songs.

One tumour is an electric storm: it shakes the Son's body like a tree. Another tumour picks him up like a pillow and doubles him over and squeezes vomit from him. The third tumour sends his eyes back into his skull looking for something. Together, the tumours take him by the throat and he can't swallow.

The Wife returns, with the indefatigable Attila. Attila

says they have come to let the truth of the Son's death colour their lives, and the Wife says nothing. No, they won't bring the Baby. This is a decision the Farm has collectively made. The Son's face is frozen now, anyway, so who knows who he knows? The Wife wipes it, and sits by him. All her hairstyles connote innocence, or Princess – Rapunzel, Hebe, coronet – and she has grown out of them, all at once, and not noticed.

More and more of The Saved gather and chant in the Day Room. The hospice complains, so Attila negotiates duties for them: vase-filling, visiting the unvisited. The Father sits among them, incongruous in his golfing jumper, helping with vases, holding his daughter-in-law's hands, conversing with Attila. He is exactly Attila's height and build, the Mother notes, their heads bend together above all the other heads, the tallest trees. The Father's eyes are constantly wet, he is tireless, the anger, as Attila points out, is all on the Mother's side.

If the Mother were more open to The Saved, and to spiritual meaning in general, she would not be so isolated. It is the Mother's choice to walk this narrow path of unbelief, and to sit alone with the Son in the depths of the night. She knows it, and when, long after language started to leave him, she hears the Son say: What people forget when they are afraid of dying is that when you die, you are ill. So you don't mind really. Being ill is shit, she tells no one. After all, maybe he didn't really say that. Maybe she has just internalized his response.

The Saved and the Father agree on a plan. The Wife brings the Baby to the Hospice garden. The Saved lift the Son out of bed and carry him, stiff and light as a charred log, outside. They hold him under the cherry tree and chant their mantras, the Father loudest of all on the *Om*s, while the Wife, a garland on her lovely head, helps the Baby stroke his cheeks with a bunch of blossom. The Mother watches all this from the hospice window, longing for the Baby, weeping, thinking she should have been asked.

But, when he does die, it is the Mother who is beside him. What happens is: he stops breathing and the Mother isn't frightened after all. One eye is open, and one shut, and she reaches across and closes the open one. There, now, Jonathon. The eyelid is warm and soft as a silk scarf left in the sun, but there is nothing living now in the hard round of the eyeball, not the least tick or twitch of life.

Then she stands up. Her name is Julia. It is nearly dawn. She goes out to the Day Room where her ex-husband and Attila and The Saved are sleeping, in their white robes, so many discarded petals. She was going to tell them something, the thing she has learned, but already it is draining from her, disappearing like water poured over sand, and she lets them sleep on and just sits down.

# Tunnelling to Mother

I was in Mother's lobby – geranium, shoe polish, pepper, dog – down on the doormat with my cardboard box. In went Mother's waisted duvet-coat, in went her clear plastic rain-cape, in went her belted mac. My nothing-coloured coat, she would say, with a moue, every time she buttoned it, eyeing me with an eye-pencilled eye.

But the coat was taupe, I'd tell her, it was dove, I bought it in Lewis's, it had a quality, grosgrain, faux-silk lining. Darling Cynthia, she'd say, screwing her mulberry lipstick back in its silver canister, tying a cerise silk scarf at her neck. I didn't say it wasn't useful. And she'd giggle, and, to Andrew, if he was there, which generally of course he wasn't, wink.

There were more coats under the coats: a three-quarter-length shorn lamb, its pockets full of mothballs; a summer blazer, Jaeger, pink; a tweed jacket of my father's; his bicycle cape of outdated oilskin, cracking along the folds; an evening cloak with bouclé collar, gone to holes, a layer of school blazers, stiff with ink and embroidered badges; a tiny sou'wester, printed with flowers, mine; the little collared coat to match. Then a leather jacket – not a tough black one but a soft brown one, tacky on the fingers, shiny, new. A nice leather jacket for a nice boy, a favourite boy with nut-brown hair, her own best boy. Well, it could go in the box, they all could.

Andrew wasn't there, of course, stuffing the boxes, labelling them *Oxfam* or *Recycle*, taping them down. No, Andrew had melted away, the way he rushed to football after Sunday lunch when he was a boy, the way he disappears each year from the Christmas table, shouting for his children, brandishing crackers and whoopee cushions. Another job for Cynthia: the chilling gravy to scrape from the plates, the cigarette ash heaped on a holly leaf to wobble all the way to the bin. You're still angry with Mother, Andrew said to me last Christmas, and I said, No, I'm not angry with her, and I was going to go on and explain actually what did make me angry, such as the washing-up, such as the assumption that *I* always have time, that my existence is less valid than his existence, simply because he has acquired his Black-Berry, his perfectly average spouse, his brimmingly ordinary, freckled children, and I have acquired only my life, its friends and such arrangements as can be held in my blue leather-backed notebook with its neat elastic, but already Andrew was off on his new tack, his new notion, whatever book it was he had read about, exhalation one two three, visualizing thistledown and beaches, *letting it go*. Pure selfishness. His children are grown now, and still.

There were so many coats now, I pulled them off in bunches without looking and tossed them over my arm, like harvesting bananas. I shoved them in the boxes and stacked the boxes into towers, and then into arches. I had to work hard to make a path through them, but when I had, it led to the walk-in cupboard, not the one in Mother's flat, but the one in our house, our real house in Broughton: purpose-made, high Victorian, you never saw such a cupboard. The light was shining through its tiny high window, and the clothes hung face-out on the walls, wrapped in white polythene and fluttering like angels. The calf-skinned suitcase was open on the floor, showing its pink secret lining. When we were little, Andrew and I would take off our clothes and take turns to shut each other in there, where it was crimson and silky and smelt darkly of the lavatory just after my father had been.

I had to fill the suitcase, but it was hard to pick out the right outfits, because there was only so much you could see through the plastic wrappers. I found the wedding dress, though, by lying on the floor and looking up the skirts, then the peach taffeta cocktail dress with the fascinating glittering texture, and the navy suit with the embossed sailor buttons. I needed the blue patent flats to go with that, but the shoes were in plastic bags like shower caps, like the ones they made me wear in the hospital – skate, scrape, skate down the miles of lino – in Mother's last days.

To get out of that closet, you had to go down on your hands and knees, open the triangular fire exit, and crawl through the roof space. Fortunately, I remembered how to do this from expeditions with Andrew. The important thing is to put your weight only on intermittent rafters, never on the intervening fluff, or your limbs could break through the plaster, or you might fall, legs first, into the neighbours' house, into their dining room, even their soup tureen. But on those trips with Andrew, we would have torches tied on our heads, and only apples in our knapsacks; now, besides the usual trouble with the dust and the clinging, furry texture of the insulating material, I had the boxes and the suitcase, though, having been to all that trouble, I could hardly leave them behind.

But, when I got out of there, I found Mother, sitting in her upright plush armchair, gazing out of the picture window, and I myself was standing on a peach-coloured carpet, a Wilton Silk-Texture. So I knew I must have tunnelled into the Home, because in the Home you had to choose when you signed up, the carpet of course, but also balconette or picture window, an important distinction price-wise, and we plumped for the window, as we didn't know then how long Mother had and it could have been years. Twenty years, Andrew kept saying, with antibiotics.

Well, I was considerably annoyed, seeing her there. I had been to great trouble, organizing the funeral. I had ordered a mini-bus to the crematorium, and how my niece shouted at me it should be a limousine. It was air-conditioned, I said, over and over, and it would accommodate more than just our family party, and perhaps young people did not want to think of Mother's friends, their legs and wheelchairs, but I did. Besides which, the scale of the children themselves, who would ever have thought it, but my niece turned away, her round eyes, like Andrew's, fixed on the heavens.

Naturally I said nothing of all this. My mother's hands were clasped at her chest and her eyes were lucent, like a glass of whisky in a shaft of sun: you could see to the textured bottom of them. She dropped her wrinkled eyelids down like swag blinds and I knew she meant I should sit down, but I was carrying too much stuff.

I dumped some of it on the carpet.

Look, Mother, I said. You're not going to like this, but I've been through everything, and sorted it, and decided what you need. And I would have said more but she stopped me, held her hand up flat and priestly.

Cynth, she said, I've been looking at the sky.

Fifty-five years, my mother has been telling me about the sky. She thinks she is better at looking at the sky than other people. She constantly draws attention to herself and her celestial observations. She will say, for instance: A real mackerel sky! or, Look at the swallows, busy little tailors! And often she will gasp: One to save up! And then she is prone to shut her eyes and make little swallowing motions and whisper: Who needs photographs! I take this badly: it is a reference to me, the family camera person, and I think a pointed one.

On this occasion, however, things being unusual, I went to stand beside her. I hoped particularly she would not make the mackerel remark, because this sky was not scaly, it was feathered, like the breast of a bird, blue, purple, red − not natural colours, more the shades of those dyed Chinese toy birds you find in cheap emporia, the ones with pins for eyes. My mother has a weakness for such things, such shops, and I glanced suspiciously at her, but she said nothing, nothing at all, just continued to gaze outwards with her special, spiritual expression.

I looked down and was pleased to see that my load − the cushions, the clothes, even the shoe box of keys − had resolved itself into a tortoiseshell dressing case circa 1940. My mother could carry that herself across the train platform even if there wasn't a porter. I needed to draw her attention to it.

Mother, I said. Look. Please. This is all sorted out. This is all you can have. I picked up the case by its horny handle, lifted it to eye-level.

Oh, said my mother. Oh Cynthia. But you know, you can't take it with you. Aren't I always saying that?

No Mum, I said. You never say that. Dear God. Was ever a nest as thickly feathered as yours? You have twenty-three throws, you have a hundred occasional cushions, you have fourteen dozen glass and china ornaments. *You can't take it with you.* Oh please. That's me. Me that says that.

Does it matter? said Mother. Doesn't it all come to the same?

But she had that face on, the especially kind and reasonable one, the oh-I-knew-that-all-the-time one which means that deep down she is defeated, that she acknowledges me.

So I put the dressing case down, and we both looked out of the window.

The feathered clouds had folded to the horizon, and the sky was smooth pink with sherry edges, like good velvet curtains faded in the sun. There were swallows on its silky surface, picking at it, and I braced myself for the tailor remark, but it did not come. Instead, as I watched, I saw for myself that the birds were stitching the sky. In fact, they were threading bootlaces through it, coloured bootlaces with metalled ends. The sky must have been pre-perforated with metal holes. Where the stars shone through, no doubt.

I had such a perforated card when I was small, when

I was no more than three, and I would stitch it at my mother's feet, when there was just her and me in the house. I would show her the card, and she would clap. Every time, she would applaud. Cynthia, she would say, I do not know how you achieved this, I have never seen stitches so very neat.

When I looked at my mother, now, I knew she was remembering the same thing. Her eyes were rapt; her loose old lips were shaping the words *stitches, so very neat*. Like a prayer. I sat on the floor beside her chair and leaned my head against the chair.

The great feather wings on the horizon were irradiated with scarlet now. Slowly, they fanned out over the whole dome of the sky, then refolded themselves and sank into the sea. They repeated the motion, again and again, slowly, with tension, like the legs of synchronized swimmers, and the sky they revealed and hid was that wonderful colour, that tremendous, spacious, pink. My mother spoke at last: Didn't I say, Cynthia, she said, didn't I always say, you were my own best girl? My only girl? My favourite girl?

She had. Of course she had, but those words had not arrived somehow, had not lodged themselves where they were needed. But now, as I watched this rare, grand gavotte of the heavens, those words also made their slow journey across the distance between us and coiled and bedded themselves down in my mind. Then truly I could feel my heart clench and unclench like those wings and

I could feel the valves of my veins open and the blood flood joyfully round my body, and I was so glad to have had this chance. So glad, so very glad, for her to say that; for me, after all this time, to hear it.

## Acknowledgements

'Aunt Mirrie and the Child' was broadcast on BBC Radio 4, read by Hannah Gordon.

'Irene' was first published in the *Observer* newspaper.

'The Book Instead' was Highly Commended in the Commonwealth Writers Competition 2011 and broadcast on the BBC World Service.

'Brunty Country' was commissioned by the Asham Anthology for 2011 and published in the collection *Something Was There* (Virago) as 'The Real Story'.

'Bride Hill' was commissioned by Ra Page for Comma Press and published in the *Litmus* anthology.

'The Not-Dead and The Saved' was the winner of the V. S. Pritchett Award for 2009 and was published in the *RSL Magazine* and *Prospect Magazine*. The story was also the winner of the BBC National Short Story Prize for 2009 and was published in the BBC Anthology of that year.

I am very grateful for all these commissions and awards and for permission to reprint the stories.

I am also very grateful to Matthew Reynolds and Kate Harvey for their perspicuous edits, and to Gill Coleridge, Zoe Waldie, Lexie Hamblin and Paul Baggaley for their faith in my work.